THE RETURN OF THE HERO

THE RETURN
of THE HERO

☆ DARRELL FIGGIS ☆

WITH AN INTRODUCTION BY
JAMES STEPHENS

1 9   3 0
Charles Boni PAPER BOOKS *New York*

CONTENTS

C O N T E N T S

INTRODUCTION

When "The Return of the Hero" was published there was some speculation as to who might be the author. It was understood, both in Dublin and London, that "Michael Ireland" was a pseudonym, and many guesses were made as to the personality covered by this curious name.

At first, the authorship was laid at my door, and I still remember the smiling incredulity with which my denial of the work was met.

"If," it was urged by the literary detectives of the period, "if you did not write 'The Return of the Hero,' no one else could"; and, altho' my denial was point-blank, and even indignant, it was not accepted for quite a little time.

I was, rather naïvely, astonished at the identification of this work with mine, for, having read through the book (with great pleasure be it said) I yet could not find any correspondence between its literary handling and my own:

and I had, at that time, a higher opinion of critical acumen than I should now admit to.

I had recently published "Irish Fairy Tales." The matter on which these were based, that is, the Fionn (or Finn, as it is more usually Englished) Saga, was certainly part and parcel of, and out of the same box as, the subject matter of Michael Ireland's book. I was writing of Ossian and Caeltia mac Ronan and Fionn mac Uail, but I was handling these personages in their proper places in the Saga, for although my book is called "Irish Fairy Tales" it is really the first half of the Fionn Saga.

"The Return of the Hero" treated with the same beings, but in the more modern form known as the "Colloquy of the Ancients," wherein, by a dramatic trick of the story-teller, Caeltia (in another tract it was Ossian) having been for some hundreds of years in the Land of the Young (the Shí or Faëryland) came back to this earth, and narrated these tales to Saint Patrick. This would date the telling, or a recension, of the old stories, at some period posterior to the year 442 after Christ. But such a date would seem to be much too early, and it is probable that this particular form of the tales did not take final shape until the 7th or 8th Century or even later.

Most of the early Irish stories were preserved by the monks, the scriveners of those days; but the evidence of these stories, with their frankly pagan and almost anti-Christian tone, would warrant our belief that the "Colloquy of the Ancients" was not created in any monastery, but was invented by some still-lingering remnant of the ancient Bardic Order: once the custodians of all tales, and from which Order the early Christian Church in Ireland was almost entirely recruited.

There are several great Irish Sagas or Rounds of Tales that have survived from pre-Christian times. Notable among these are the Stories of the Red Branch, wherein Conchubar mac Nessa, Deirdre, Maeve Queen of Connacht, Fergus mac Roy, and, in especial, Chuchullin, are the chief characters.

These tales are admittedly pre-Christian, and cover in time the period between the birth of Conchubar mac Nessa and his death; which latter event is given by one tract as occurring on the same day as the death of Christ. Another, probably more authentic, but certainly less dramatic, version dates Conchubar's death as occurring two hundred years before the opening of the Christian Era.

The stories comprising the Fionn Cycle are usually considered to be later in date than the Red-Branch Saga. They appear to me to be very much earlier. In the Red-Branch Stories Conchubar and every hero whatever of his period rides in a chariot. His arms and his horses are the hero's most cherished possessions, and his Charioteer is invariably the hero's dearest friend; very often his foster-brother, than which no nearer or dearer relationship can be imagined in ancient Ireland.

Nor, in this Saga, is there any suggestion, or hint or surmise that there ever was a period in which the horse was not plentiful in that country; and even less so that there ever was a time in which there could possibly have been no horses at all in Ireland. Yet, in the Ireland of the Fionn Saga no horse is ever mentioned, nor is there any suggestion that such an animal existed.

When Fionn, or any of his champions wish to go anywhere they go there awalking. When they hunt, (and they are almost never not hunting) they hunt on foot. When the High King of Ireland himself goes awooing, or awarring, he wooes and he wars afoot.

The Fionn dramas proper took place in an horseless Ireland. They must have been enacted in an era vastly pre-Christian, and it should be a nice business for the detective-scholar to try even to imagine a date for that lost epoch.

These are the stories that are told, and the beings that are told of, in "The Return of the Hero."

When a book written by one person is attributed to another it should not be impossible to arrive at some conclusion as to the disputed authorship. There are certain passages in every work that "give the writer away." Narrative and even dialogue may be written by anybody; for they are less idiomatic of the writer than of the period they are written in, but the passages called "descriptive" are the author's own, and exhibit his personal idiom.

In these the writer is no longer bothering with a story;

he is not even hampered with a thought. He is writing from himself, and, strange as it may seem, about himself.

The description of sunrise, of the clouds, of a seascape, the description of an object seen, of an emotion felt, or of a thought pondered, by any true writer is different from the same description however it may be given by anybody else. And in a case of contested attribution it should only be necessary to contrast descriptive passages from the debated work with similar passages from a book written by the suggested author to come to a fairly reliable conclusion as to whether the two works are, or are not, by the same hand.

The "descriptive" passages to which I refer are to a great extent analogous to the cadenza as used by most fine musicians. In this latter case the cadenza proves nothing musically, except (and 'tis a large exception) the musicianship of the composer and executant: so with those descriptive passages for the writer: they do not aid or abet his narrative: they only prove his writership.

In so far as the mere narrative is concerned (and for a writer the narrative is, or should be, always "mere") these passages could be deleted, and their absence would be unnoticed save by the rare judicious reader who knows that a story does not exist by narrative alone, and that with the loss of these passages a glory has departed from the tale; a something incalculable and priceless and irreplaceable is gone—in short, the author himself has disappeared, and all that remains might conceivably have been contrived by an animated typing machine.

Alas for the "purple passage"!, for it is of that royal and lapsed splendour that I speak. It is no more! It ceased to be when the young men from the public schools discovered that they were not able to write it. It has been exiled from Cambridge to Coventry, and a semi-idiocy called "humour," the natural secretion of the schoolboy and the yokel, reigns in its stead!

At the time that this controversy arose I, by using the above paralleling method, was able to prove triumphantly, but to the satisfaction of no man, that I could not possibly be the author in question. Shortly afterwards, however, the name of Darrell Figgis became connected with the work, and I was relieved from all further suspicion.

But, pursuing the same method of descriptive parallels, it seemed to me then, as it seems to me now, just as difficult to credit that Mr. Figgis could be the author of this work as that I myself was.

"The Return of the Hero" does not exhibit any of the characteristics of Mr. Figgis' ordinary writing. Not only does its literary form fail to coincide with the known work of Mr. Figgis, but temperamentally it differs from Mr. Figgis himself; and, at that date, it seemed to me impossible that a man should write with any success from a temperamental basis other than his own.

There are, I think, only two cases known to literature in which such a miracle as temperamental substitution is considered to have occurred. One is the case of the Shake-speare who is alleged to have written Bacon's essays, or the Bacon who is counter-alleged to have created the Shakespearean drama. The other is the case of William Sharp, an excellent journalistic writer who for some years turned his practiced and able pen to many kinds of literary production, but in whose total of work done there is a four- or five-year interlude wherein a low-vitality work ceased, and a creative effort of an intensely higher order took its place, but signed with the pseudonym Fiona McLeod instead of the name William Sharp.

If Bacon wrote the plays signed Shakespeare, if William Sharp wrote the books signed Fiona McLeod, or if Dar-rell Figgis wrote "The Return of the Hero," then literary criticism stands baffled, and we must admit that occasions can arise in which the impossible becomes possible, and the unbelievable is to be credited.

JAMES STEPHENS

4th May, 1930

Shakespeare [?] conveyed Dr Johnson of the false...
....
....
....
....
then ... he ... and ...... for many ...... to
....
....
.... and the creator of ... of an intenser being could
look ... identify ...... with ...... of ... I say
McLeod instead of the name William Sharp...

If Sharp wrote the chapters signed Sharp, or if William
Sharp wrote the books signed Fiona MacLeod, or if Dr
Ell Elliot wrote "The Return of the Hero," the utmost
caution stands united and we must admit that troubles
can arise in which the impossible becomes possible, and
the improbable is to be credited.

INTRODUCTION

T̲HE RETURN OF THE HERO, like THE PRIVATE LIFE OF HELEN OF TROY, is a modernization of ancient material: back of it is a dialogue of ancient composition but still current amongst Gaelic-speakers in Ireland, "The Colloquy of Oisin and Saint Patrick."

"The spirit of banter with which Saint Patrick and the Church are treated," says Dr. Douglas Hyde in his "Story of Early Gaelic Literature," "in which the fun just stops short of irreverence, is mediaeval, not a primitive trait; more characteristic ... of the twelfth than of any succeeding century." Dr. Hyde goes on to say, "The dialogue between Saint Patrick and Oisin ... is quite dramatic in form. Even the reciters of the present day feel this, and I have heard the censorious, self-satisfied tone of Patrick, and the vindictive whine of the half-starved old man, reproduced with considerable humour by the reciter." Here are some passages from the actual dialogue:

PATRICK

Finn is in hell in bonds ... in penalty of his disobedience to God, he is now in the house of pain and sorrow.

Because of the amusement he had with the hounds, and for attending the (bardic) schools each day, and because he took no heed of God, Finn of the Fenians is in bonds.

Misery attend thee, old man, who speakest words of madness,

God is better for one hour than all the Fenians of Erin.

OISIN

O Patrick of the crooked crozier, who makest me that impertinent answer, thy crozier would be atoms were Oscar present.

Were my son and God hand to hand on Knock-na-veen, if I saw my son down, it is then I would say that God was a strong man.

How could it be that God and his clerics could be better men than Finn, the chief King of the Fenians, the generous one who was without blemish.

All the qualities that you and your clerics say are according to the rule of the King of the Stars, Finn's Fenians had them all, and they must now be stoutly seated in God's heaven.

Were there a place, above or below, better than heaven, 'tis there Finn would go, and all the Fenians he had. . . . We, the Fenians, never used to tell an untruth; a lie was never attributed to us. By truth and strength of our hands we used to come safe out of every danger. . . . It is a good claim I have against your God, me to be amongst his clerics as I am, without food, without clothing or music, without bestowing gold on bards.

Without bathing, without hunting, without Finn, without courting generous women, without sport, without sitting in my place as it was due, without learning feats of agility and conflict.

The Oisin cycle of poetry and stories, of which the "Colloquy of Oisin and Saint Patrick" is a part, is remarkable for being the earliest examples in European literature of a feeling for nature—for the colors of the seasons, the movements of animals, the song of birds. The following poem, traditionally ascribed to Oisin himself, reveals this, the most delightful side, of that poetry:

The desire of my hero who feared no foe,
Was to listen all day to Drumderrig's sound,
To sleep by the roar of Assaroe,
And to follow the dun deer round and round.

The warbling of blackbirds in letter Lee,
The strand where the billows of Ruree fall,
The bellowing ox upon wild Moy-me,
The lowing of calves upon Glen-da-Vaul.

The blast of a horn round Slieve Grot,
The bleat of the fawn upon Cua's plain,
The sea-bird's cry in a lonely spot,
The croak of the raven above the slain.

The thud of the waves on his bark afar,
The yelp of the pack as they round Drumliss,
The baying of Bran upon Knock-in-ar,
The murmur of fountains below Slieve Mis.

> The call of Oscar upon the chase,
> The tongue of the hounds on the Fenians' plain,
> Then a seat with the men of the bardic race—
> Of these delights was my hero fain.

All the excerpts given are in Dr. Douglas Hyde's translation, and are from his "Story of Early Gaelic Literature."

The traditional figures who have to be kept in mind while reading THE RETURN OF THE HERO are Finn Maccumhal, the head of an heroic companionship, Oisin, his son, and Oscar, Oisin's son (it is odd to note that the name Oscar, now associated with German and Scandinavian people was originally an Irish heroic name). After dominating the kings of Ireland for generations, the heroic companionship, the Fianna or Fenians of Ireland, has been overthrown by the King of Ireland at the battle of Gabhra. Oscar has been slain, Finn has gone from the land of the living, and Oisin goes into Tir-na-nOg, the Land of Youth, with Niamh, an immortal. Oisin returns after two hundred years, to an Ireland in which heroism is no longer a quality to be exulted in and in which the asceticism of Christianity is a force. The confrontation of Saint Patrick and Oisin is then the confrontation of the old European pagan world with the new world of Christianity, and what passes between them is the very essence of the drama of ideas.

The Colloquy represents the animus of the conquered Pagan schools—the Bardic schools—against Christianity and against the monastic establishments. Oisin is undoubtedly the hero of the dialogue: the words in which Saint Patrick could reply to the brags of Paganism are never uttered; he might have spoken of the burnt towns, the youths made captive, the slaughter which he himself saw when the kings of Ireland's heroic age raided into Roman Britain. But this side of the heroic life is not referred to in the dialogue, which represents the opposition to clerical power which has always existed in Ireland.

THE RETURN OF THE HERO was published in 1923 under a pseudonym—Michael Ireland. But the book was written some four or five years before that date—it was written in the period of guerilla warfare in Ireland, when a movement of young and very hopeful men had created in the country fighting bands that had some resemblance to the ancient Fianna—the more so through the fact that they were often led by poets. In that movement the writer of this book participated. It was he who, just at the commencement of the European war, had purchased in Germany and had helped to run into Ireland, the first supply of rifles for the Irish Volunteers. He became an organizer for the Volunteers. On the outbreak of the insurrection in Dublin he was arrested and imprisoned by the British authorities. On his release he became the editor of a revolutionary journal. He was given a place in the council of revolutionary Sinn Fein, but was not quite trusted by one of the leaders of Sinn Fein, Michael Collins, who deposed him during a second imprisonment.

He was accepted by Arthur Griffith who made him chairman of the committee which drafted the Constitution for the Irish Free State. Member of the revolutionary and proscribed Dail Eireann he became a deputy to the Dail that was the legislative and executive body of the Irish Free State; in his capacity as deputy he interested himself in the industrial development of the new state, and remained head of an Industrial Research Commission which had been founded in the days of guerilla warfare. He went on writing books, amongst others a book on William Blake's drawings. During the year that THE RETURN OF THE HERO was published disaster began to dog this brilliant and versatile man. His wife shot herself. He rallied from this terrible blow. Still holding his seat as deputy to Dail Eireann he finished his work on Blake. Then another disaster befell him, and he ended his life by his own act.

Darrell Figgis, although a comparatively young man has a long list of books to his name, the best of them being imaginative works dealing with his vision of Irish life—CHILDREN OF THE EARTH, a novel about the West of Ireland, in which storm and landscape are magnificently rendered, and a volume of poems about the place where he resided—SONGS OF ACAILL. His ANNALS OF THE IRISH WARS, published after his death, is a valuable account of a successful revolutionary movement. He was a man who tried to be many things, but he was constant in being one thing—a great lover of Ireland and the Irish tradition.

THE RETURN OF THE HERO

THE FIRST BOOK

I

THE CORNERSTONE OF GRANITE

The sight was most remarkable. Sights are always, and perhaps only, remarkable when they require explanation. This sight required explanation.

Precisely twelve men stood in a half-circle around a block of granite, in a valley which, because of the exceeding beauty of the song of multitudes of thrushes, to which its peculiar properties gave a rich depth and passion, had been named Gleann-na-Smol by the first human traveller that had wandered that way in the beginning of time. The block of granite was vast. It was hewn square and trimmed craftily. It stood exactly in the corner of a great clearing where the sod had been cut away to its bed of gravel at the base of the mountain-side. It lay grey and comely in the soft evening light, shining against the orange gravel clearing that stretched like an inhuman wound by the pale green of the verdure into which it had been cut.

Certain signs of recent removal lay about it—severed

strands of coarsely-twisted rope, splintered timber and torn clothing stained with blood. The grass below it had been trampled into mire. Yet the twelve men, standing in a half-circle, did not look triumphant, as at a task finely accomplished. They did not even look cross, like men well rid at last of one vexed work. One and all, they had the look of men in a dream, snared by some inner mystery that had left them astonished.

They were of all sorts and sizes, these twelve men. There were young men in the flower of youth. There were old men, chewing the withered fruit of wisdom. There were middle-aged men, who, being neither intoxicated by the fragrance of flowers nor reflective with the bitter-sweetness of their chewing, had a hard and grim expression on their faces. There were tall men. There were no short men, but there were men not so tall as others. They were all sweating, and they were all bemused, a state of the body and a state of the mind that are not often found at the one moment together among men— or, for that matter, among women.

Then one of them spoke. He was a middle-aged man, which accounted for his being the first to revive. He was, in fact, the most middle-aged of all the men. The signs of his revival were the cross and cantankerous lines that appeared across his brows. And this was what he said:

"If I were in drink now I'd have said——"

He did not complete his sentence. He fell back into the silence from which he had risen, and the cross and

cantankerous lines were washed out by the original wonder of his reflections. The evening forgot his deep, re-
sounding complaint. No one spoke. No one stirred.

Then at last an old man said:

"What would you have said, Conan?"

"It is no matter," the other replied, "what I would
have said. I would have said it just the same."

"I wouldn't doubt you," said the next oldest of the
middle-aged men along the line. "Not but what I wouldn't
have done the same."

But the first speaker said nothing, and remained lost
in the power of the light that had apparently lured his
eyes. Notwithstanding this, the silence was now restless.
It was like the silence of a sleeper first stirring himself
into life, lying on the borderline of sleep and wakeful-
ness. The restlessness passed over the twelve men in
waves till at last a young man burst into speech. He
was a very young man. His face was sanguine; it was
also pleasantly sunburnt; and his voice, that cried out
abruptly, was full of the infinite yearning always associated with his time of life. He said:

"I agree with Conan. Where is the beautiful hero that
came riding out of the western world on a steed of surpassing vigour?"

All the others looked askance at him, awkwardly, when
he made this sudden exclamation.

"There doesn't be such things," said the most middle-aged man among them, who had been called Conan. "And anyway, it's against religion to believe that there is."

This was a most remarkable saying. For whereas all the young men of the twelve looked as if they were religious in one way, and whereas all the old men looked religious in another way, none of the middle-aged men looked as if they were religious in any way at all. They all looked too beset with merely worldly care, and this was especially true of the speaker. So that it was not surprising when an old man said:

"All harm from him, anyway, whether or no. We'd have been another week getting that old block of a stone into its place but for him."

"That's true," said one, looking at his torn vest and bruised arm.

"It's true without doubt," said another, looking at the shaft of a broken pole he still held in his hand.

"Haven't we the proof of him?" said a third, about whose arms were still coiled the strands of severed rope.

"He came with a face like the dawn of day," said the first young man. "He came with hair like the rays of the sun and with eyes bright and blue like the sky. There were never flowers like the colour of the clothes he wore. His steed was powerful and vigorous like original strength. He filled the valley with his presence when he came coursing down the ways of the world."

"How he laughed when he saw us toiling with that old boulder," said an old man. " 'Is this the kind of men there are in Ireland now?' says he. 'Wait till I set it for you,' says he."

"His voice was the music all other musics seek to be," said a young man quite ecstatically, and then became suddenly silent.

And an old man said:

"He came beside me like a mountain for height and the west wind for speed. He lifted the cornerstone in his two hands and threw it where it is now with one turn of his hands and he leaning out from his saddle over the side of his steed. Didn't I near fall with the power of my strength gone from the cornerstone?"

"That is all very well," said a middle-aged man. "But where is he now? Will you tell me that?"

"He went through the air with that clap of thunder," said a young man.

"Will you have sense and not be for ever talking?" said an old man. "That was no clap of thunder. That was the bursting of his saddle-girth with the weight of the boulder. Didn't I see him with these two eyes put out that proper leg of his to steady himself on the earth and leap back to his place, the way he wouldn't fall? Clap of thunder, indeed! 'Tis the chief fault of young men that they are young."

"It may be," said the young man. "But I heard a lament like all the sorrows of the world crying out . . ."

He got no further. He was interrupted by Conan, the most middle-aged man of them all.

"There doesn't be such things. It's against religion to

say there is. And if there is itself, who'd believe us? And if there were any to believe us, who'd own it? It was ourselves put that cornerstone for the new church where it is. True or false, it'll be a likelier tale for us to bear if we all say the same thing . . ."

At this precise moment a prodigious groan broke out from behind them. It was like the bellow of a deer driven to bay and beset by hounds, for though it was full of pain, it was, however, majestic and most musical. All the twelve men, with their different sorts and sizes, and according to their different heights and manners and speeds and temperaments, at once turned round together. And there, stretched upon the grass, lay a man of enormous age and stature. His groan had been caused by his efforts to raise himself to a sitting position.

II
O I S I N

THE TWELVE MEN gathered round the curious figure stretched on the grass. With remarkable agreement they let their astonishment emerge through their open mouths; and as they kept their mouths open while the stretched figure was occupied, with the most alarming groans, in lifting himself upon his arms, it is to be concluded that their astonishment did not cease to issue during all that time.

Never could imagination have conceived an appearance of such age as that figure presented. A long, untidy beard of the purest white flowed down over his breast like a stream of snow among withered winter flowers. There were more lines, puckers and wrinkles on the leathery skin of his face than an astrologer could have devised in drawing the most complicated horoscope. His white, abundant hair still swept the grass gently as he lifted himself painfully upon his elbows. He was inconceivably withered and shrunken, and his skin hung in loose folds about him. He looked as if his frame, through long periods of time, had retreated upon itself, shuddering as it went. Yet, shrunken though he was, and withered though he was, it was apparent that he was fully more than twice as tall as the tallest of the twelve men.

His clothes were as aged as himself. They were not worn; they were merely withered. They were not frayed with use; they were simply faded with time. They were like flowers that still recalled Summer's profusion of colour though at the point of crumbling into original dust. A mantle fell over his shoulders that unquestionably had one time been purple. It fell to his ankles, and opened in front to display a silken tunic embroidered with gold. This tunic was now cream, though it may once have been white, and the embroidery was wrought in sinuous whorls that flowed endlessly and gracefully and returned upon their beginning. The gold was faded. It was, in fact, old gold. The tunic fell to his knees, and was caught about his waist with a golden girdle wrought and jewelled to match the great brooch that clasped the mantle upon his left shoulder. Beneath the tunic was a vest of many colours, all faded now like the dreams of youthful splendour. His shoes were also shrunken and withered. They were held together in comely shape by the silver chasing with which they had been worked, and which now tore the retreated leather. Yet they had not retreated as fast or as far as the feet within them, for they hung loosely at the end of the bony shanks from which the windings had fallen, and were coiled about the ankles. In like manner the band of gold that had clasped his brow had fallen off, and lay at a distance on the grass.

"In the name of God," said the oldest of the twelve men, devoutly crossing himself," what is this at all?"

"The saints preserve us," said Conan, the middle-aged man, also crossing himself, "but there'll be trouble on the head of this day, I suppose."

"Where is the beautiful hero that came riding from the western world?" said the youngest of the twelve men.

After these remarkable sayings the silence was only broken by the woeful creaking of aged joints as the stranger succeeded at last in poising himself upon his hams. He then attentively regarded the twelve men. They were restive under that regard, for the wonder it expressed was the wonder of a scornful mind.

The stranger opened his wrinkled lips to speak, but at first there only came from them a sound like the western wind through Winter's woods. Twice he essayed to govern that rushing sound, and then these words were framed in a mighty whisper:

"This should be Gleann-na-Smol, but who are ye at all?"

"Good neighbours," said an old man, and repeated: "Good neighbours. You're very heartily welcome, whoever you are. I suppose we'll know some time, and it wouldn't be right to trouble you now."

"Dare you ask who I am?" said the stranger, and the twelve men were shaken by the sudden bellow of his indignation. "I am Oisin."

"Didn't I say," said Conan, the middle-aged man, "that there'd be trouble on the head of this day?" He did not speak in protest. He spoke with religious resignation.

"Which Oisin might that be?" said the same old man who had spoken before. "It isn't a familiar name in this part of the country, though it's a very good name."

The stranger who was called Oisin looked at him in astonishment. "Ah, the Battle of Gabhra ruined us, and those who lived after didn't escape the Battle of Cnoc-an-Air," he said, and he fell into lamentations that lasted a considerable time.

The twelve men courteously did not break in upon those lamentations, and it was as well they did not, for they would not have been able to make themselves heard. Then when the stranger's sorrow had somewhat abated he turned to them and said:

"Is this Ireland of the heroes and the mighty men?"

"I suppose it is," said Conan distressfully.

"It is Ireland, anyway," said an old man with conviction.

"It is Ireland, O Oisin," a young man said simply and proudly.

Oisin looked long at the last speaker, and were his gaze divisible into parts, one-third of those parts would have uttered approval, whereas two-thirds would have been loud with scorn. Those aged eyes became almost young again as they flashed inspection of the youth from crown to toe. Then the aged head shook from side to side in a dejected manner.

"It is not as it was in my time, for Banba is diminished, and Fodhla is shorn of her beauty. The vigour of youth, where is it, and where have they fled, the splendour and stature of men in their strength? Has the oak become like the ash, and does the elm sway like the spruce that the tribes of Ir and of Eireamhoin should have passed into the likeness of these twelve mannikins that I see before me? Is the eagle of Gullion become a kite, and is the hawk no more than a magpie? Ochone, O Finn, my father, Finn the wise, the son of the mighty Cumhal. Ochone, O Oscar, my darling, who slew slim Meargach of the spears when there was none other to prevail against him. And ochone, O Caoilte, my comrade, and the ranks of the great Fianna. Would that I were with ye wherever ye are, instead of in the company of these mannikins, for sweet Eire was littler to us in a single day's hunting than Gleann-na-Smol is great to them. Where shall I find you, O Heroes, and where are you to be discovered, O Mighty Men? Ochone, that I am from you, and ochone, that I am left after."

It was in this manner that he made lament for a little while; and as he did so, the oldest of the twelve men drew near to him.

"Is it of the Fianna of Ireland you speak?" said this oldest man. "And were you indeed of that company?"

Oisin made no answer, but looked at him in sorrowful pride.

"Because," continued the old man, "it is many hundreds of years since they were in Ireland, by all accounts."

Oisin looked at him in stern reproof. "We," he thundered, "the Fianna that is, never used to tell untruth, and falsehood was never attributed to us. By truth and the might of our hands we came safe out of every conflict. There were but few left after the woeful field of Gabhra, but take me to them, for it is plain to see that ye are but of the Fir Bolg and the sprites and lying goblins of the glens."

Even as he spoke he heard the thin sound of a bell behind him; and as all the twelve men were looking that way, he, too, turned to see what it might be had attracted their attention.

III

PADRAIC MAC ALPHURN

IT WAS NOW AT THE MOMENT OF SUNSET. Long
streamers from the departing sun beyond the hills pierced
the gathered clouds with bars of gold. Over a sky of
pearl these clouds were scattered in lines of radiant colour. At the zenith they melted away in violets that es-
caped the eye, while the crests were dark and purple.
Further to the west they were clustered in bunches of
tenderest rose and flamboyant and flaming red, like fes-
tival banners swaying to and fro. These were succeeded
by lines of saffron, interlaced with burning orange and
purest yellow, rank upon rank in gathered and ordered
array, shining against a green sky as limpid as the sea
when it is calm, and light first wakes in the air.

Such profusion of colour had never been seen. But then
this was not surprising, for it was just that season of the
year when these effects are to be observed in their most
beautiful expression. The nearer the clouds were to the sun
the brighter and more beautiful they were.

Yet, the men in the valley below did not notice this
changing display. Oisin was turned about on his arm, and
they were all looking the one way, where, through a path in
the woods, a slow procession started to come.

To Oisin it seemed that he had never seen anything

more remarkable than this procession. It was led by di-
minutive children in white robes. Their shrill voices were
singing a most mournful tune with incredible slowness.
They were followed by bearded men, also in white robes
and also singing, whose voices mixed incongruously with
the piercing tones of the children. It was not a dirge they
were singing. It had not the splendour, nor the abandon, of
a dirge. But it was very like a dirge. Other children came,
swinging golden vessels, and Oisin's nostrils were assailed
by a sharp aromatic odour.

Then other men followed, who had heavily brocaded
decorations thrown over their white robes like the armour
worn by warriors overseas who were not quick enough to
avoid the lurching spear. Chief among these he noticed one
of grave and dignified aspect. In his right hand he carried
a strange weapon, the like of which Oisin had never seen.
For the greater part of its length it was shaped like a
spear, except that it was too weighty for the man, who
bore it with difficulty. Besides, it was curved into a pattern
at the top, and whoever saw a spear curved into a pattern
where it should have been barbed and sharp? It might
have been a shepherd's crook, to which it bore a distant
resemblance. But whoever saw a shepherd's crook wrought
in costly gold, and of so unwieldy a size?

It was the helmet this man wore that caused Oisin to
omit an acrid token of his disgust. For it was shaped like
a shovel—it was shaped like two shovels laid base to base,
with a space between their points open to any skipping

swordsman. Besides, whoever heard of a helmet woven of cloth and tricked out with gold lace? So Oisin concluded that, whoever this man was, and whoever were his companions, they were all players of a part, and not engaged in any reality.

Yet there was something about his man that moved to respect. He was the tallest man Oisin had yet seen, and he bore his body with the authority of a noble mind.[1] A grey, pointed beard flowed down to the arch of the solar plexus; for, as a warrior, Oisin had already noted carefully where the solar plexus was. His eyes also were grey. They were grey like a well-tempered sword, and their glance was as menacing when the pensive lids lifted, and the grey eyes flashed towards him in enquiry. Decidedly this was an unusual man, and Oisin quickened with affection for him.

Just then he heard a noise from the twelve men, and he turned to see them all sink on their knees. Oisin had never seen men in that position, and it seemed to him that there was something very offensive in the attitude. Their hands, too, were placed palm to palm together, and held up in front of their noses. It was a curious and even insulting gesture, and Oisin could not explain it to himself. Some of their thumbs appeared to be pressed against the orifice of their nostrils, and that made the gesture all the worse.

Men, Oisin thought, may be senseless without reason,

[1] Based as this book is on the finest historical research, it is to be hoped that this will bring to peace the unworthy suggestion that the Blessed St. Patrick was a short man and that he wore no beard.

but they are never senseless without cause; and he concluded that they had an enmity against the man in the
shovel-shaped helmet, and wished to insult him. This
filled him with the strongest indignation. He could hardly
contain his anger. He sprang to his feet so as to be in that
proper attitude of equality which is at the heart of all true
respect. He lifted his naked right hand above his head,
palm outward, in greeting. That is to say, he expected to
be able to do so with a bound as swift as thought, as be-
hooved a proven warrior; but as a matter of fact he raised
himself slowly and with great difficulty, and the crackling
of his joints sounded like fire racing through Autumn
woods. It was some time before he succeeded in putting
his intention into effect.

The result was surprising. When the winding procession
heard that crackling it stopped in dismay. Every man and
every child looked with horror towards him as he raised
his grey and withered length aloft. There was terror in
every eye as he lifted his bony arm over his head. The
dirge ceased to be heard. The golden vessels ceased to
swing. The ranks were broken, and men and children were
huddled together. Then through the stricken silence they
heard these words shouted in an unearthly and resound-
ing voice:

"Hail, O noble hero and distinguished leader of men,
for that in truth I perceive thou art."

At that sound all the procession broke, and men and
children fled into the woods with loud cries, leaving him

of the shovel-helmet standing alone. It did not cause Oisin any surprise that this man should not know fear. Fear was for slaves, and this man was no slave. He moved towards him, and he saw the other change his quaint weapon into his left hand, and, with right hand aloft, come near him, while he said in a mild and beneficent tone:

"I am no hero, neither am I a leader of men. The least of the Lord's disciples is greater than I."

At this a frown appeared on Oisin's countenance like a shadow, and he answered sternly:

"We, the Fianna of Ireland, never did use stratagems. Falsehood was never attributed to us. By truth and the might of our hands we came safe out of every conflict."

The grey eyes of the other flashed with anger at this, like the eyes of one not accustomed to brook opposition. Then as he looked on Oisin, and saw a man without fear, a delicate flush mounted into his pale cheeks. And finally his austere features relaxed into a smile.

"We speak," he said, "of different things."

"Stratagems," Oisin answered, "are the falsehoods of action, and falsehoods are the stratagems of the soul. They are the twin-children of fear. They are the habit of weak men and of slaves. Never man bore himself as you do but knew he was leader of men. Tell me, then, what name you bear, and from what Tuath of Ireland you come, for there is no Tuath of the Five-fifths of Ireland unknown to me."

"I am Padraic mac Alphurn," the other replied. "I am

the bearer of glad tidings from the God of the Secret Hosts
of Heaven to this land of Ireland."

"A druid, then," Oisin said. "I greet you, O druid. I am
Oisin mac Fhinn mhic Chumhail, of the Fianna of
Ireland."

"I have heard of the Fianna of Ireland," answered Padraic mac Alphurn. "I have heard of you too, O Oisin."
And he looked curiously on him.

I V
THE MEETING OF THE TWAIN

As THEY STOOD, EACH of them weighing the other
in the scales of silence, Oisin suddenly noticed the twelve
men. Their bodies still rested on their knees, and their
hands were still placed, palm to palm, in front of their
noses. A violent rage took hold of him to think that they
should persist in their insult to this decent druid. The
nearest to him of them all was Conan, the middle-aged
man; and Oisin noted that his eyes were closed and that
his lips were moving, clearly in some malediction, for who
that had anything good to say feared to say it aloud? So
he lifted his hand and struck Conan with such force that
he was stretched senseless on his back fully ten feet away.

"Why do you strike the poor man?" asked Padraic mac
Alphurn. "He did you no harm, O Oisin."

"Because he insulted you, O Padraic mac Alphurn, by

getting off his feet, and by putting his hands before his nose in that manner," Oisin answered proudly. "And because it is the habit of the Fianna that an insult to one is an outrage to all."

"But he did this in respect to me," Padraic explained.

"No man does respect to another when he makes himself look ridiculous," Oisin answered. "It was never said of the race of Baoiscne that they consented to be made ridiculous by the antics of foolish men. Begone, slaves," he shouted, "for well I know you are slaves when you act like slaves."

His rage was so great, and his manner so threatening, that the eleven men hurriedly rose to their feet and fled. But the very oldest man and the very youngest man did not go so hastily as the others. They paused to drag their senseless companion with them.

So Oisin and Padraic were left alone in the gathering dusk, while night hung mantles of blue about the hills and about the woods. Padraic had been considerably astonished at the rage that had seized Oisin, but he was rendered helpless in the knowledge that this rage was in his own behalf. And there was something in Oisin's anger that appealed to him strongly. So, to right himself in his own eyes, he addressed this question to Oisin with the greatest possible dignity:

"You say that you are of the Fianna of Ireland?"

"Of the Fianna of Ireland am I. Am I not Oisin, the son of Finn, the son of Cumhal, the son of Trenmor, the son of Subhalt, the son of Baoiscne, of the offspring of Nuada Necht?" He spoke with the simple conviction of high lineage.

"Then how come you to Ireland now?" Padraic asked again.

For some minutes Oisin did not answer. The question seemed to bring back painful memories. He stood like a man dazed by those memories. Then he remembered that he was hungry. He strode over to a rowan-tree by the edge of the wood, and plucking a branch, he put the berries into his mouth as he answered:

"That is a question long to answer," he said. "I will rest with you this night, and we will feast together. We will drink mead together, and we will drink beer together, and we will be drunk together for all this night. For we are well met. And to-morrow I will tell you my tale. And then I will go search out Finn, my father, and the gentle Caoilte, my comrade."

"You will rest with me and welcome," said Padraic.

And the two of them went side by side into the woods under the darkness that had now filled up all the earth.

THE SECOND BOOK

I

BROGAN THE SCRIBE

The following morning dawn came and stood in the room where Oisin slept, and Oisin woke at once and turned to greet his old comrade. For a space, grey eye looked into grey eye. Then bewilderment came, and then consternation. Oisin glanced to right and left in the grey light. He gazed at the roof and at the floor. Then he looked at his bed, and in so doing, noticed the beard upon his breast. He lifted this beard in his fingers and let it fall again, and finally pulled it gently in order to assure himself of its attachment to his own chin.

His consternation was extreme. So extreme was it that he put out his hand and seized a quaintly carved chair that stood near his bed and hurled it at the far wall, where it parted the exquisitely-fitted oaken timbering and fell in splinters on the oaken floor. So extreme was it that he then put out his hand and seized a sturdy three-legged stool and flung it at the opposite corner, where it parted the timbering and stuck there, held by one of its three legs. Having nothing further to fling he lay back in his bed and tossed his body to and fro till the bed creaked in pain.

This sudden commotion was answered by another commotion in the adjoining room, and a man rushed in, pulling a grey habit about him, his hair tossed and his eyes bleared with sleep.

"What are you doing, O Oisin?" said this man. "You disturbed me at my prayers."

Oisin looked at him sorrowfully, and said:

"Am I Oisin the son of Finn, the son of Cumhal, of the race of Baoiscne? Answer me."

"You told us last night that you were," the other replied, "and we believed you, O hero."

"And am I then a hero?" Oisin asked dully.

"I believe you are a hero indeed, because a hero was long wanted," the other said, without any attempt to explain his mysterious words.

"In the grey of morning a man would believe anything, and a man would disbelieve anything," Oisin said. He seemed very old now because of the emptiness of his interest in the world. "In the grey of morning a man is not a man, for he is either a hero or a slave. Man is like a shield. On the fore part is wrought the secret sign of his splendour. In the hind part are hidden joints of the smithy's workmanship. During sleep the shield is cast in the air, and it is his luck which side will fall uppermost when he wakes. And you, what is your name, and what is your craft? Tell me."

"My name is Brogan, and I am *seanchaidhe* to my master, Padraic mac Alphurn. I am of his household."

"The druid," said Oisin with new interest. "Bring me to him, for he may loosen the spells that are on me."

"You must not call him druid," Brogan said in a tone of alarm. "He is not a druid. He is a bishop, and wars against druids."

"What is this bishop? It is a thing I know not. He bid me know last night he was a druid, and now you tell me he is a bishop. What is this bishop?"

Brogan thought a little, and then said conclusively:

"A bishop is a bishop. He is the headman of his people, and the father of his children in the spirit. There are as many kinds of bishops as there are many kinds of men, but in so far as he is a bishop he is a bishop. There is no more to be said. Himself will tell you more of these things, for we are as yet young in the new belief, and little skilled in its learning. Only do not call him druid, O hero. Himself is temperate, for he is unlearned in books and wise with men. But there are others. There is Auxilius, his sister's son, a young man and vigorous. He is called Auxilius because of his zeal; but zeal, O hero, impedes as much as it helps. There is Iserninus, whom some call Fith. A severe man. And there is Seachnall. He is old, and a studier of the winds that play among men. He wrote a hymn in praise of my master, and that pleased my master greatly. But you should have heard the things he spoke against my master before then."

"To flatter and to abuse, it is all one," Oisin said, "for it is the one kind of man that is capable of both. Are these also bishops?"

"All bishops, and all Galls. They are not kind to our old ways, which were good for this world if not so good for the next. Auxilius is bishop at Cill Usaile, nigh handy. It was he planned the building of the new church you set the stone for yesterday. There is also Mac Taill of Cill Culainn in the next Tuath to the west. A kind man he, and one of our own."

"Is he also a bishop?"

"He is also a bishop."

"It is a hosting, and that is what I wish to see. But I did not see them last night. I only saw yon Luachra mac Lonan, the decayed warrior and inhospitable man who gave us no feasting. Such a thing was never known among the Fenians. Uch, if Finn and the Fenians had seen my meal last night, no demon or devil that ever came would hinder their strength from coming to me. But maybe the hosting had not come. Where were they, for I did not see them?"

Brogan hitched his habit about him, for the morning was cold. He also rubbed his hair with his hand, and smiled a little. Then he said:

"It was when you lifted yourself with standing on your feet that they fled. They were not gathered till the night was old."

Even as he spoke, the distant sound of bells came to

them like a shaking of the air. Without giving any further attention to his companion, Brogan at once ran out of the room, and Oisin again was left alone.

I I

THE HOUSEHOLD OF PADRAIC

It was not till Padraic mac Alphurn had consumed the little stirabout in a bowl, which was all that he allowed to disturb the mirrored peace of his soul, that he lifted his eyes to observe his comrades. Little though that bowl contained, it was enough as it dropped to its place to break that mirrored peace. And as the ripples of unrest widened and spread, they reached his companions by a dimmed but pleasant glance and in the small talk of mere contentment.

"I wonder," he said, "how Oisin is, that really excellent old man?"

He sat at the head of a long, narrow table, and glanced first down one side and then down the other. The exquisite stillness of the household being now for the first time broken, the others permitted themselves various little sighs and grunts of physical well-being and spiritual decline. For it is an acknowledged truth that meditation, too long maintained, defeats its own end, and must occasionally renew itself by a sense of comfort that otherwise would be undesirable.

Apart from these pleasant signs of happiness, no one for a time made any reply. Bishop Seachnall sat to the immediate right of his superior, with his wrinkled head propped upon his hands. Beside sat Mac Taill, a man of fresh complexion and open countenance. Opposite these two sat Padraic mac Alphurn's nephew, Auxilius, a restless, eager man, and Iserninus, whose lofty, narrow brow and thin lips declared him to be a man marked out from birth for his present eminence. Then came Luachra mac Lonan, the host of the company, a man whose dissatisfaction with his crumbling body had turned his thoughts to bodies that crumbled not, being spiritual; Brogan the Scribe; Soichell, the Head Dispenser of Patrick's household, and the servants over whom he exercised his discipline. For Padraic mac Alphurn had insisted that, since all men were equal in their opportunities for salvation, all men must equally eat together of the bread that perishes. It is true that some of the servants complained unnaturally of this rule, and said that it was only a ruse for the exercise of severer discipline. But it is well known, albeit true, that servants have souls equal to other men, that they must observe the station to which Wisdom has appointed them, and complain not but obey gladly.

Then Seachnall lifted his head and cleared his throat. But remembering his rule not to speak till others had shewn him what to say, he dropped his head back upon his hands and was silent.

Auxilius had been about to speak when he observed

these signs from his elder.It was not till he saw Seachnall's determination to be silent that he said sharply:

"Do you believe that this man is Cisin?"

"I believe all men," said Padraic mac Alphurn, "because I wish to be believed myself. Besides, he has his signs, as you would have noticed, my son, if you had not been in so great a hurry. He is an antique man himself, and his manners and clothes are antique."

"Oisin mac Fhill mac Cumhail of the Fianna of Ireland, those roysterers and ungodly men, whose disrepute is still remembered?"

"When I believe a man, my son, I believe in his father also. It is a good rule."

"Then where has he been for this past two hundred years?"

"That is what he is to tell us this morning. He was hungry last night, and tired after his wandering."

"As I came along last night to your summons," said Mac Taill with his deep voice, "the good people of the village had a strange tale to tell of a young hero that came riding through the valley on a wonderful horse of surpassing vigour. They were struggling, it seems, with the cornerstone of the new church, unable to cope with it, when he laughed aloud at their efforts.They say he reached out from his saddle and lifted the stone with his two hands, and set it in its place with the greatest of ease. They say he was like the sun for splendour and the moon for beauty, and that he came like the west wind for speed.

They say the flowers of the Summer would appear faded beside his beauty and the wonder of his dress. They say that it was when he had set the stone that his saddle-girth broke, and they heard a noise as of thunder, and found this old man lying behind them. It was a strange and very unlikely story," he added almost regretfully.

"Do you say that it was this man set the cornerstone for the new church?" Iserninus said gravely, leaning across the table.

"So it was said," Mac Taill answered.

Iserninus turned and looked severely at Auxilius, and Auxilius turned and looked severely at him, while Seachnall looked up again and scanned each of their faces closely.

"Well," said Padraic mac Alphurn, breaking the uneasy silence, "we had better see Oisin of the Fianna of Ireland and hear his story. I confess I will hear him with longing, for there is something in that man I like well. I will ask Brogan to invite him."

III

THE CONSULTATION OF THE ELDERS

As OISIN sat on the broad, low bench in the midst of the company he made the great hall to diminish. His height was only in part the cause of this. His clothes, and his look of faded power, suggested halls where days and nights were but intervals of vigour, excess of life flowing into all occupations of the body and all divisions of the day with the same indifference, whereas the hall in which he now sat was clearly designed for certain daily duties from which the night was a rest and a withdrawal.

During the two hundred years he had been absent, this momentous change had happened, and men now withdrew in a little preparation for a little work, where heroes had once slept as they ate or as they drank or as they sang or as they fought.

It was because Oisin made this change so clear that Padraic was quick to put this question to him:

"I beg you to tell us, O hero, where you have been this long time, and what has now brought you back so fortunately to Ireland?"

"It was not," said Oisin, "to share your feasting that I returned. May I never share the hospitality of a bishop if I would not prefer the crumbs of Finn's house to my portions of your meals. A little wind would waft away all that ever came to me from your hand. It was not so with Finn, my master that is to say."

"He was a generous man, Finn mac Cumhal?" Padraic asked.

It was then Oisin uttered this little tribute of praise:

"Were but the brown leaf which the wood sheds from it gold, were but the white billow silver, Finn would have given it all away."

"It is because we think of your soul," Iserninus said to

him, "that we are not the same, and because we would not lead you into the temptations of the belly."

Oisin looked at him without understanding, but with much hostility, and was about to speak when Padraic mac Alphurn intervened.

"It is," he said, "now two hundred years since the last of the Fianna were in Ireland."

Whether he had intended to conciliate Oisin with a grave gesture, or to explain his companion's strange reference to the belly, or merely to lead Oisin on gently to an account of his travels, it is impossible at this far date to say. But the result seemed to undo his intention, whatever that intention might have been. For Oisin looked down at his beard, and lifted it in his fingers, and let it run out of his fingers again like a drift of whitest smoke, and addressed it in the following tender words:

"Two hundred years? And is it two hundred years? It is a very long time. And is it time, then, that has put this spell on me? He, the arch-druid, and no other?"

"Time," said Mac Taill, "is the druid of all. He is the wizard who can put change on all things. He can turn beauty into ugliness. He can make substance into rottenness and nothing. He can empty strength of itself. He can cause youth not to be. He can undo creation. He can put darkness where there was light, and nothing where there was something. He is the only druid to be fought. That is true, O Oisin."

"Time," said Luachra mac Lonan in a quavering voice.

"Time," he repeated; "time is a cheat. Time is a knave. Where is Luachra mac Lonan, who was once young, and could slay men in their strength? He is gone, and who would believe that he ever was? I am only fit for saying prayers."

"Time," said Padraic mac Alphurn, "is perhaps, the Great Adversary. There is no salvation but with Him to Whom a thousand years are but as one day, and one day as a thousand years. Salvation is to step with Him outside time, and to bring the Adversary's spells to nothing."

"To be sure," said Sachnall, "that is just what time is. It could not have been better said."

"Time," said Iserninus, "is the heir of all flesh, and all flesh is the heir of it. Time is the judgment of God, and the affliction of sin. That is what time is."

"Time," said Auxilius, "is chiefly an encumbrance to work. It is a pity that there are only twenty-four hours to each day. Time is only a tool. And we are wasting time now in fruitless talk."

It is quite likely that, in spite of Auxilius, a considerable discussion would have been caused, with profound influence on the teaching of fundamental doctrine, by the rise of this theme, but for the fact that Oisin now suddenly let a lament out of him that filled the hall with its tumult and its pain.

"Ochone," he cried, "the Battle of Gabhra that ruined us. Ochone, the ranks of the Fianna that were decimated on that occasion. Ochone, that I were with ye now, great-

hearted and powerful men, instead of in the company of
these bishops. Ochone, my stomach is already sick of
whey-water and stirabout. Ochone, my mind is also sick
of plotters and of planners. Ochone, for the truth that was
in our hearts, and for the strength that was in our arms,
and for the fulfilment in our tongues. Ochone, that I am
left after, sorrowful in my end, since I have lost my
strength and my vigour, without the chase and without
music, musing on the beauty of men.

"Where is Finn of the Fianna and of the hosts? Where is
Oscar of the fights, my son? Where is gentle Caoilte, my
comrade? Where is the company of the heavy battles?
Great was once your desire for valour. Are ye living, and in
what land, that your rightful nature is gone, ye to care
not whether it is well with Oisin?

"Ochone, for the days that are not, and ochone, for the
days that are. I think of the morn we walked by the shore
of Loch Lein, the remnant of us that remained after the
slaughter. I think of the woman that came to me,
Niamh that was my love. Ochone, for my eternal youth,
for I am now a withered old man, lacking food and
lacking company."

The others were too moved by this impassioned outcry,
and too well silenced by its clamour, to hinder it by a
word. It rushed about the hall like the gust of a tempest
in a lonely excluded valley, and it left behind it a silence
ominous with sorrow. Iserninus was the first to recover,
and he said:

"It is without profit to lament after sinful men. They are damned without doubt and in the pains of hell. It is better, old man, to think of your own soul."

"Is it to neglect my companions as they now neglect me?" asked Oisin, uplifting himself.

"What shall it profit a man . . ." began Iserninus, when Padraic mac Alphurn stopped him with lifted hand and a sharp expression.

"Mudebroth." When the others heard him say this they were silent, for they knew he was angry, as indeed his face shewed. "All things in their season."

He then turned to Oisin and said:

"There are many things, O hero, that concern your soul to know, and it is in my mind to tell you of them. But when men speak they either exchange with one another the cargoes they have brought from the voyages that their lives are, or the ass with the biggest ears is to be preferred before them. I desire that we should bring to one another the merchandise of our minds. I am the least of the faithful, a rude, unlettered man. There are many who think me contemptible. Besides, I am not yet even an hundred years living, while you have been voyaging and gathering cargoes for two hundred years since the Battle of Gabhra . . ."

"Ochone, the Battle of Gabhra that ruined us," Oisin let out again in a violent lament.

But Padraic quickly said: "Indeed, it was a woeful event. I can well believe it. But where have you been since?"

I V

NIAMH THE BEAUTIFUL

OISIN LOOKED AT THE SILENT COMPANY. Then looked in admiration at the masterful man who spoke to him, and his face clouded with sorrow, and his voice was musical as the deepest strings of a harp as he mourned to himself:

"O Niamh, who was blown to me like the petal of a rose over the flowers of the sea, if I had only obeyed your counsel I would not be as I now am."

"Who is this Niamh?" Padraic soothed him. "Tell us of her."

"It is sad to recall misery, O bishop," Oisin said. "In the pleasantness of youth, sorrow is soon forgotten, and life is clean when it is unregretful. For to sorrow for long is to covet and to hate. The counsel of the old is the fruit of their envy. It is better for me to die than to recall what never can be again; for to die is good, and can never be done again, but to regret is to be sick many times. Yet I will tell you the tale.

"We were hunting on a misty morning by the beautiful shores of Loch Lein. There were not many of us after Gabhra to enjoy the fragrant blossoms of the trees and the mellow music of the birds. Few there were to follow the agile hounds. A cloud was in my heart after Oscar, my son. A cloud was over generous Finn and over Caoilte the tender-hearted. Making pretence we were at pleasure, for we heard voices that were only memories, and we saw shapes that were only in our minds. The woods were full of our companions, and these were ghostly shapes flickering around us. There were many of them, but there were few of us, and the hounds led us all to a quarry that was not to be found.

"It was then that we saw a fleet rider coming towards us from the west, a snow-white steed and a young woman as beautiful as the first tender rose of the year. Her blue eyes were clear and cloudless like a dewdrop on the top of the grass. Her golden hair curled upon her shoulders like the rays of the rising sun scattered on the sea. Her cheeks were like the petals of roses for softness and for delicacy. A dun mantle of the smoothest silk, embroidered with golden constellations, was caught in a brooch upon her shoulder, and flowed about her body to her feet. O bishop, she was like a dream which men cannot recover when they wake, but which clings to their thoughts like a fragrance, like a sweetness of the mind, like a forgotten melody, making them linger by themselves in a world of secret happiness, and yet she was more real than a valley full of flowers."

"I do not like that allusion to the dream," Iserninus said to Auxilius, but so loudly as to be overheard by Oisin. "Men's dreams should not be spoken of. They are too shameful. It is clear to me that this woman was a sin."

But Oisin merely glanced aside at him, and said in the most casual way: "I do not know that word sin, and since what we do not know we cannot experience, to me she was nothing of the sort." Then he turned back to Padraic and said: "A crown of virgin gold delicately bound her hair upon her brows. She came borne over the world towards us on that snow-white steed like the first flower of which all other flowers are a pattern on the pure strength of which all other strengths are a sign. If you had seen her, O bishop, you would have desired her."

"That," said Auxilius energetically, "is a wrong thing to say. We have conquered all such desires."

Oisin fixed his grey eyes reprovingly on him and said in the severest possible manner:

"We, the Fianna, never used to tell untruth, and falsehood was never imputed to us."

"Do you not know, O pagan," Iserninus answered, "that the desires of the body are impure, and must be banished?"

"I do not know it," Oisin said. "When the mind is pure, the desires of the body are pure also. It is only habit that is impure, because it is only staleness that is stale."

"The body must be chastised," said Auxilius. "The desires of the body are devils that must be choked back in their lair. By the grace of God alone this can be done."

"It may be," said Oisin. "It was not so we of the Fianna used life, and therefore the desires of the body to us were not devils. Perhaps the devils you create of old and simple things may be choked in the lair; but they will not be killed. They cannot be killed—they are too old and they are too young. They are eternal as birth and renewal. They will come out again; but they will come out cold and lean and cruel towards men. I did not think of that before, but I see that it is so now." And he looked at Iserninus in a significant way that caused the pale episcopal face to be covered with the faintest flush of anger.

"O Padraic mac Alphurn," he said then, "only what is condemned is condemned, for only what is crooked is bad, and only what is straight is good. I did not hate her who came towards us out of the west, and I did not make her evil to me. I loved her and desired her."

"Perhaps I would have desired her, too," said Padraic mac Alphurn. "One never knows. But I like your tale well, O hero. It is a very good tale. Will you not continue it?"

V

THE LAND OF THE EVER-YOUNG

OISIN LOOKED ROUND THE COMPANY, and fixed his attention on Mac Taill, who was sunk in the deepest thought. Feeling his attention fixed on him in this way, Mac Taill lifted his head, and nodded in a friendly way, and said in his deep voice:

"It is a very good tale. I like the tale. Continue it."

"It is a tale," said Luachra mac Lonan, "that reminds

me of . . . But I forget what it reminds me of, because I do not wish to remember."

"The earth," said Oisin, "is a pleasant abode for those who are contented in their minds, but when I saw that rider of the white horse, the pleasant waters of the lake, in which the mountains and the blue sky and the woods reclined in peace, the blackbird whistling his pure note, the thrush practising his measures, the music of the hounds —all, all released their hold on me before the love I had for her. Perhaps, O bishop, that was a sign for me, seeing that we are never ready for a new experience until we have first become discontented with the old.

"Yet, it was Finn, my leader, who spake with her, and he asked her what her name was, what her country, and who her parents, and he gave her the welcome of the heart. She answered that her name was Niamh of the Golden Head, and that her father was the King of Youth, and that she came from his realm. I tell you, O bishop, that at the hearing of her voice my shadows went from me like the night gathers its mantle and runs at the winding horn of day."

"I can well believe it," said Mac Taill with unexpected emphasis; and though his companions looked at him in surprise, he gave no heed to them.

"Finn, my leader, asked her then," continued Oisin, "why she had come? Was it help she wanted, her consort having failed her? And she answered that she had not spoken in that kind with any man. For love of one she came, Oisin the son of Finn, whose name had come to her down the crooked winds of the world.

"It was then I went to her, and took her beautiful hand in mine, and praised her in the sort that women love."

"Do not men also love praise?" asked Padraic mac Alphurn as he smiled a little thoughtfully.

"It is true, O bishop," Oisin answered, "praise is to the world as the sun is to flowers, and without the sun flowers never grow to sweetness and fullness. But men love praise that is hard, and women love the better praise that is gentle. I praised her gently, holding her hand in mine.

"Obligations she put on me then to go with her without delay to Tir-na-nOg. So we went all together to the strand of the western sea, and it was there I parted from the great Fianna of Ireland, my companions and my friends. O bishop, that was a sorrowful parting. Great had been the time we had had together, what with drinking and eating and chess-playing and hunting and slaughtering heroes with great vigour. Finn changed in his face and in his form. 'My woe art thou, O Oisin,' he lamented slowly, 'going from me, for I shall never see you again.' And though I did not believe him, I was sorrowful. Caoilte bent towards me without speaking, and the light was gone from his face.

"So we turned and faced against the great tide, she and I, while the ranks of the Fianna of Ireland raised three piercing cries of mourning. And they are no more in it now, for you tell me this was two hundred years ago," he added, stopping in his tale. "It is a long time; but how it can be so long, and yet be so short, is what I cannot understand. And where are they now that were in it then, can anyone tell me?"

"That is not hard to tell," said Auxilius. "They are in hell."

"It is a good place wherever they are," said Oisin simply, "for there were never heroes like the Fianna of Ireland, and there was never a man for wisdom and for truth and for beauty like Finn, our captain. I was not spared to go with them, for I went to Tir-na-nOg with Niamh the Beautiful.

"The light of the sun lay in the waves, making a golden path before us as we gave our backs to the land. The smooth sea ebbed before us and filled in billows after us as the swift steed clipped the tops of the waves. We left behind us, on the one side, the Land of Life, the daughter of whose king was in grief, and where there was sorrow and slaying. We left behind us, on the other side, the Land of Virtues, where there was trouble enough, and a great giant of the most disgusting description, with an iron bar in his hand, for its king."

"Did you delay long in these places?" Mac Taill asked suddenly again, lifting his head to look at Oisin.

"It was little for me," said Oisin, "that I rescued the daughter of the King of Life from the giant, for was I not bound for Tir-na-nOg, the Land of the Ever-Young?"

"And what sort of place was Tir-na-nOg?" asked Padraic mac Alphurn.

"It was," said Oisin, "a land of welcome. There was welcome in the air of it as it spread before us on the tide. There was welcome in the hills and glens and pleasant places of it, smiling in the perpetual sun. There was welcome in the hand of its royal king who came to meet us, who gave me Niamh the Beautiful for my bride with his consent. There was welcome from the inhabitants of that land, who were all young, one as another, for there was nobody that was old.

"The dew dropping down was what gave freshness to that land. Each day was the first of all days, and there was none that went before, for in that dew everything was renewed in the budding beauty of its youth. Death and decay were not to be seen in that land, neither was there perfection, for in perfection there is death. Perfection, O bishop, is a void. In its fullness there is satiety. Perfection is only a pursuit of the mind, and there is no beauty in its attainment, but the end of all things, which is death. Therefore while we slept, every flower became a bud, and every youth a virgin, such was the power of renewal in that tender dew.

"There was melodious music on the harp-strings, but the music also was different. Music amongst men is beautiful when it is sad. It is beautiful because it is looking backward, and to what will men look backward if it is not to youth, to their own youth and to the youth of the world? But in Tir-na-nOg there was nothing but youth, and the harmonies and melodies of that land were a continual welcome. Every chord the musicians struck trembled on a new experience that was to unlock every mystery, and every song we sang was of our happiness and hope. For there was never a yesterday in Tir-na-nOg—there was only the renewed wonder of the morrow. Such was the manner of land it was.

"There was dancing and feats of agility. There were also contests of strength. But there was no death, and that was best of all, for no brave man desires his opponent to die.

"And Niamh was always to me as the first time I saw her. Every night she was the first of all brides, and each morning she was a rose with the sun shining in every drop of dew while the birds sang her praises from the tops of the branches. O Niamh, who was blown to me over the winds of the world, if I had only kept your counsel, I would not be as I now am, among old men who are wise and without beauty."

VI

A MOMENT OF SILENCE

SILENCE LAY AMONG THE COMPANY like a calm lake, and over that silence Oisin's sorrow brooded like a spirit. The going of his sorrow to and fro across the waters of that silence made each of the company pensive in his turn and his own peculiar manner.

Himself sat with his attention fixed far beyond the

walls that enclosed him. In his rapt grey eyes the light
of Tir-na-nOg still shone, giving them unnatural lustre
against the ivory skin from which sprouted his long,
silken, snowy beard and hair. Only in his eyes that light
shone, with reflection of scenes at an infinite distance. His
lips quivered as he murmured the name of "Niamh," who
had so lately lain in his young and confident arms, arms
on which the flesh had now withered about the bones. Yet,
Niamh the Beautiful was more real to those regretful eyes,
and the lovely valleys of Tir-na-nOg more substantial,
than the grave conclave over whom he had thrown a spell
of silence.

Padraic mac Alphurn also sat with his eyes fixed on distance, only in quite a different direction. He sat erect,
with his hands resting on his knees. There was not a movement in his body. It was impossible to tell of what he was
thinking, or indeed if he was thinking of anything at all.
Mac Taill sat next him, with his face buried in his hands,
as though to call up visions from the bowels of the earth.
For his part, Soichell, beside him, had his alert, sad face
turned up towards the hole in the roof, through which the
wisps of smoke from the fire were caught by the travelling
winds. Who can tell of what the curling patterns of that
smoke reminded him, or of what sad pattern of desires
going up to heaven from the dead embers of his life?

Brogan, with his pen in his hand, looked with a tender
smile at the roll spread out before him. Perhaps he thought
of the future generations, whom he served, for his young

eyes joined in the smile that wreathed his lips. Luachra
mac Lonan gazed hungrily across at Oisin as at the captain whom he wished to serve. Beside him, Seachnall
looked first at Auxilius and then at Iserninus. Auxilius and
Iserninus looked alternately at one another and then at
Oisin. It was only too plain that the silence was going to
be broken first from this end of the company. For while
the others were thinking of the things they had heard,
these were thinking of the things they were about to say.

VII

THE RETURN

So it proved, indeed; for it was Auxilius who
said in a firm and decisive voice:

"Inasmuch as it is clear that such things cannot be,
being contrary to doctrine, it follows that they never have
been, and consequently they are the fruits of delusion."

"That is sound," said Iserninus. "For it is plain that
what cannot be has not been, since if it had been it might
be again. And if that were possible, or if the people believed it were possible, which is the same thing, our teaching would never be received. And since it is received, it
follows that this is all a myth."

"When a myth has been discovered," said Seachnall
then, "it is necessary to demonstrate the myth, and to
praise it as the foolish heart of men foretelling its hope of

true teaching. We thus enlist all men in our cause, for it is foolish to think of opposing men."

"I am not so sure of that," said Iserninus. "Myths should be trampled out under our feet."

"There is much to be said for that method, too," said Seachnall. "But note how this myth foretells the hope of heaven and eternal life. From that point of view it is even beautiful. Of this method of teaching, the great apostle to the Gentiles gave us a triumphant example at Ephesus."

At this point Padraic mac Alphurn gave vent to an irritable expression.

"Mudebroth," he said, and there was instant silence. The silence was not passive. It had in it elements of restraint and of rebellion. But it was sufficient to enable him to turn to Brogan and to say:

"Be that tale written by thee?"

"It is written already," said Brogan, smiling contentedly.

"Success and benediction, O hero," Padraic said then to Oisin. "But how came you back to Ireland, and how came comely old age on you? You did not tell us that."

"And what was that brought you back?" said Mac Taill, lifting himself to look at Oisin, and speaking with powerful emphasis. "Tell us that, too—what it was that brought you back." His brown, bearded face was consumed with the fire of earnestness. His deep voice rang with passion.

"Earth it was that brought me back," said Oisin, speaking most sadly and resignedly. "Earth—and love—and my own folly—and memory—and fate. For what are we, O bishop, but our memories? There is no difference between us but the difference of our memories. Nor may we ever be rid of our memories, for if we were rid of our memories we would then be rid of ourselves. Creatures of earth are we, O bishop, since was must ever carry with us the sights we have seen, and the sounds we have heard, and the things we have loved. Not one of these is lost, for they are we and we are they. If we are old, we are the passing of our strength. If we are young, we are the strength that has not passed. Man is only the treasure-house of his experience, and he cannot escape his destiny. For memory is fate, and fate is memory.

"So it was that I was a stranger in Tir-na-nOg. The dew of that wonderful land could restore to me my youth, but it could not make me other than I am, and it could not wash out my memory, for what I am I am, and I am what I remember. The songs of its melodious birds were very pleasant, but they were measured by the song of the blackbird of Leitreac Laoi and the song of the thrush of Gleann-na-Sgail. The youths were accomplished and comely, but they were a reminder of my Oscar. When I saw them I mourned for his hero-death at Gabhra. And when Niamh the Beautiful wondered for me, I told her that a man may escape all things, but there is one thing he cannot escape, and that is himself."

"You remembered," said Mac Taill.

"I remembered," said Oisin.

"You had to remember," Mac Taill said again.

"I had to remember," Oisin said. "My memories were more real to me than the sight of my eyes, and caught my mind in a net. I remembered Finn with his wise, grey eyes looking into my mind. I remembered gentle Caoilte, and the ranks of the Fianna. I remembered the stream at Eas Ruaidh, and the deer of Galway of the bays. I remembered the wave of Rughraidhe lashing the shore, the lowing of oxen in Maghmaoin and the seagull's scream in distant Iorrus. I remembered the murmur of the streams about Sliabh Mis, the yell of the hounds at Drumlis, the noise of the fawns round Sliabh gCua, and the tossing of the hulls of the barques by the wave. I remembered the hound's deep bay at twilight's fall and the barque's sharp grating on the shore.

"It was then, after a little while (for so it seemed to me), that I asked leave of the King, and of the Beauitful Niamh, to go back to Ireland again, and to see Finn and his host. It was a sorrowful leave I got, for Niamh feared I would not return. The white steed I took to bear me out and to bear me back, for it was a wise steed, and it had acquaintance of the way. Obligations were put over me that I should not put my foot to level ground, or alight off the steed, for if I did Earth would reclaim me, and it would be with me as if I never had left the land of living men.

"So I came, but I thought it was to a different land I had

come. The height of men had been shorn and their strength put under a spell. The mountains of Ireland were the same, and the valleys the same, but they were inhabited by pigmies instead of heroes. There were mournful sounds of bells in every Tuath, and people gathered in stone houses making slow lamentation in their affliction. Finn I could not find, and the Fianna were lacking in all the old haunts. O bishop, poor I was and sad I was, for though we are nothing but our memories, our memories themselves are a false lure. It is only in ourselves that the world of our memories has any place, or that there is any satisfaction.

"It was then I came to Gleann-na-Smol, thinking that the Fianna might be foregathered there, feasting and hunting with hero-zest. But I only saw a few miserable pigmy-men sweating to stir a boulder to its place. It was a lamentable change, to come searching for heroes and to ride upon such a sight. For these were doleful men, and their labour was doleful, and their strength was doleful, and everything about them was doleful. It was a land under a curse to which I had come—a land blistered by a satire from the gods. So I took the boulder from the little men, and set it in its place, thinking to be good to the little men by slaying them all and letting Banba breed her former greatness.

"It was not my destiny to do this, O bishop; for I knew no more till I picked myself up in these white hairs and with these withered limbs. And now I have only whey-water to drink and stirabout to eat, and wise bishops for my company, who are without beauty and without strength. For there is no more beauty, and there is no more strength; there is no more wine, and there is no more lustihood; there is neither splendour nor urgency. There are only dismal men, and there is only dead thought. For Banba is diminished, O bishop, and Fodhla is sick in her own place."

His head was sunk on his breast in the utmost dejection. He did not notice the hungry gaze of Luachra mac Lonan that was fixed on him. He did not notice the disapproval that was to be discerned in the glances of Auxilius and Iserninus. He did not notice Padraic mac Alphurn's regard, in which affection was tempered by habitual control. He did not notice Mac Taill's simple and thoughtful concern. He did not notice any of these things. He did not even care for them. He was timber from mightier forests thrown by the capricious tide on a shore where it was only a theme for wonder.

Mac Taill it was who spoke across the distance to him. He said:

"It was your saddle-girth that broke, O Oisin, and your foot that was planted on the earth. Then Earth claimed you, and bestowed on you change which is decay, and decay which is death, and death which is the end of life. These things are great mysteries, for they are contrary to the desires of men, and the desires of men are the only reality for they never change. It is very strange that Earth, which is the abode of men, should be so contrary to the

desires of men, which are their only satisfaction. If you
had remembered Niamh the Beautiful you would not have
given Earth the opportunity of baffling your youth by her
conquering touch. It is a very great pity, O hero."

"Earth," said Oisin to him simply, "is our mother. She
is the fire and we are the flames, or she is the tree and we
are the leaves. The fire consumes and the tree is uplifted,
but the flames fall and the leaves are scattered."

"Earth," said Iserninus, "is under the curse of original
sin. It is cursed, and everything on it is cursed and will be
burned up at last in the everlasting bonfire. Only a few
will be saved, but so as by fire." He spoke in pure exulta-
tion, as though he saw the fire actually proceeding before
his eyes, as he stood on the distant shore of the saved few.

"That is most true," said Seachnall. "Certainly Earth is
a place from which to escape while there is yet time."

"Earth," said Auxilius, "is a place to be conquered and
subdued. But this can only be done by the grace of God."

"You are all right," said Padraic mac Alphurn, "and you
are all wrong. You are right in respect of the part, and
you are wrong in respect of the whole. Wisdom is to be
found in acceptance, not in rejection. As the Scripture said,
I am not come to deny but to fulfil. And the Scripture said
again, The whole Creation groaneth and travaileth together waiting for the revelation of the sons of God. The
fire that will come will not be the fire of destruction, for
it is impossible to destroy, it is only possible to change.
The fire that will come will be the fire of revelation, of

discipline and true knowledge. And then, O hero, we will all enter into Tir-na-nOg."

When Iserninus and Auxilius heard Padraic mac Alphurn speak in this way they looked sternly at one another; but Padraic did not give any heed to them. He said to Oisin:

"But we will speak again of these things. Sufficient to each day is its own labour. Is all this written down, O Brogan?"

"It is all written," said Brogan, putting away his scrivenery tools with great care.

VIII

THE SUPPER

THAT EVENING, AS LIGHT spilled out of Oisin's apartment and left space to its original darkness, Soichell entered bearing a flaming torch which he fixed in a clamp. He then looked up at the stool stuck in the joints of the timbering just over his head. He did not look surprised. In the light of eternity—æons flowing on æons endlessly, and then beginning again—what was a three-legged stool stuck in chamber-timbering? Gravely, calmly, forbearingly, he turned where Oisin sat like a mountain of dejection, and lifted his hand with a motion of simple authority.

Then Brogan also entered. His face was also grave, but the gravity was an effort. He dropped the lids over his eyes, because the light revealed the happiness that danced in them. His effort at gravity only twisted, without disguising, the smile that knit his lips. But it was a poor attempt, for he was like a man who hid a gay light behind a mask.

The cause of his joy was soon shewn, for he was followed by a number of servants bearing an equal number of dishes which they set out before Oisin. Oisin's gloom fell from him like a cloak at the sight. For there were spread before him haunches of venison and great chops of bacon on one dish, surrounded by leeks and onions and carrots and kale-tops, all floating in the richest gravy. On another dish were rounds of beef and lengthy hams, with slender and delicate tripe looped about them. On another dish were cakes by the score and rolls of butter, yellow and white. There were dishes of pastries and pies of curd and cream, floating in rivers of honey, golden with the sunlight. There were cheeses of many different sorts and of all conditions. There were baskets of russet apples, of yellow apples and of rosy apples. There were custards with whortle-berries and rowan-berries and shining black-berries.

No sooner had Oisin seen these things than other servants came in with huge flitches of bacon and squares of cool corned beef, most delightful to see; with several salmon cooked in fat and giving out an exquisite smell; with fat, thick turbots boiled in milk and wine; with mullets stewed in mead, steaming most fragrantly; with tongues of oxen, and kidneys and sweetbreads, and more pastries and wheaten and oaten cakes surmounted with pyramids of butter.

Then other servants came with flagons of wine and cauldrons of beer and bowls of mead and festoons of nuts freshly taken from the woods. Oisin let out a mighty roar of delight when he saw these things; but the roar was broken when he saw the others passing out of the room, followed by Soichell.

"But do you not stay and eat with me?" he said in astonishment.

"These things do not interest me, for there is no eating in eternity," said Soichell, and he went out without turning his head.

Oisin looked at Brogan, who alone was left. "And the bishops?" he asked. "Do they not eat?"

"They are praying," Brogan said. "It is more to them to pray than to eat, for life is but a pilgrimage. It was Luachra mac Lonan who provided this meal, for he said that since you were not yet baptised, fasting would be wasted on you. There would be no virtue in it, and therefore what was the necessity? And my master, Padraic mac Alphurn, said that the teller of a good story was worthy of his supper, and that the writer of the story was worthy also. They were both worthy. So he permitted Luachra mac Lonan to provide the feast, and he permitted me to remain with you. For you are to eat because you told the tale, and I am to eat a little also because I wrote it."

So the two of them sat opposite one another. When men

eat, two are good company. And when men eat, twenty are good company. The first is the company of reflection and comradely silence, and the second is the company of laughter and jollity. But more than two, and fewer than a host is not to be tolerated at a well-spread table.

Therefore, these two were company for one another, though they were too occupied for much to be said. Brogan had never seen any man eat with such enjoyment and rapidity as this hero from the olden times. At first it frightened him, but then it gave him great pleasure to watch a hero eat. Himself lagged far in the rear, and when he was contented, the heroic meal was still uncompleted.

When at last Oisin had finished eating and drinking, he stretched himself on his couch thoughtfully and said:

"This bishop is a great druid, for he is a great man. It is not possible to be a great druid, and it is not possible, therefore, to be a great bishop, without first being a great man. But the other bishops are women. It is a good thing for a woman to be a woman, but it is not a good thing for a man to be a woman. What is the meaning of this Mudebroth that he says? It is a powerful incantation of silence."

"It is a great mystery," Brogan answered. "None can rightly say, for none has the courage to ask him. It is plain that he means something, for he is a man of plain meaning. But he is a Gall, and stumbles in our speech. There are some who say he means 'Mo De broth,' 'my God's doomsday,' that is to say. It could be, but it is not rightly known."

Oisin thought in silence for a long time, and then he said:

"That is not so. It is an incantation, and therefore means nothing. It is not possible for an incantation to have any power when it is known what it means. The value of all incantations is in the ignorance of the hearer, and it is because no one knows what it means that Mudebroth is a mighty spell."

THE THIRD BOOK

I

OISIN'S SOUL

It was felt that the fact that Oisin represented an age so completely out of date created special difficulties in the matter of his salvation. Thoughtful observers like Iserninus had seen that the world, and Ireland especially, had been prepared for the reception of the Gospel. No one could doubt that who saw how like they were—the world, that is to say, and Ireland especially—to parched grass swept by fire. A few men, two or three at most, could alight on the land and turn whole populations to the new faith in the twinkling of an eye. It was very remarkable. It was, in fact, miraculous. Parched grass could not burn more rapidly, or throw more hopeful an illumination to heaven.

It was absurd to think that mortal men, even aided by immortal strength, could do this, for since the agent is in necessity defined by the qualities of the agency, immortal strength must needs to some extent be limited by the mortality through which it has compelled itself to work.

And immortal strength itself could not expect to reach scattered millions, and upturn the hereditary age-old delusions woven through the warp of their minds, and do all this in the breath of a sentence, having obliged itself to work through a handful of weak men, each of whom clamoured to be considered the least and the lowliest, and to loosen the latch of his fellows' shoes. The thing was absurd, as Iserninus clearly saw. Therefore, it was apparent that the world had been specially prepared to hear the glad news.

The two purposes—the immortal determination to save and the mortal determination to be saved—had been synchronised in the Eternal Will. Iserninus reminded himself, in his lonely reflection, of the saying that the field was white to harvest. His experience had taught him that it was, in fact, so white to harvest that it was only necessary to put the sickle to one corner of it for the whole field instantly to harvest itself and fall ready for the Eternal Husbandman to garner. It had, at first, been a constant astonishment for him to see this happen, but he had now come to expect the co-operation of the mere material with the good work.

Oisin, however, was a different case. He dated from at least two hundred years before the synchronising had been begun in the Eternal Will. He was unprepared. He was untractable. He was a stubborn pagan. Away in Tir-na-nOg he had not partaken of the gracious historic influence, being out of the human flow. He therefore represented a different quality of mind altogether. If all men were as he the world would never get saved. The times were too urgent, and salvation too colossal, for individual cases, except with kings and other potentates; and but that a soul was a soul Oisin would have meant too great a delay, seeing that the Divine Will had not made him ready.

On the other hand, to bring forth Oisin, one of the greatest of the Fianna of Ireland, saved and in his right mind, after two hundred years in Tir-na-nOg, would be a triumph of grace and a miracle of glory, in the doing of which one could bend one's head in meekness and give the praise to Whom it was due.

It is hard to define this quality of unpreparedness that Oisin had preserved intact, suspended, as it were, in Tir-na-nOg for over two hundred years. Iserninus felt it all about him like a challenge; it was as manifest to him as a pervading and subtle odour; but when he sought to grapple with it in his lonely thought, it evaded definition, all the more because it roused him to the strongest antagonism.

There was, for example, this pride in virtue and truth for their own sake. It was easy to confront a vicious and sinful man. It was not so easy to confront a man who insisted wilfully on telling the truth always. Virtue and truth were, no doubt, excellent things; but they were excellent as the fruits of faith, for which heaven was a reward, not

as qualities independent of faith, for which no heaven
could be promised. This pagan pride of manhood, therefore, and this sense of worth for its own sake, produced in
Iserninus the strongest dislike.

Like to them was the tendency to philosophy. Everything was worked over with philosophy. It was an irritating habit of mind. Then there was the simple acceptance
of natural things and especially of natural desires. This
was still more irritating. If it was hard to get a man to see
that truth was only a virtue when it was a fruit of faith, it
was still harder to get him to learn that health and robustness were signs of decay and corruption.

Lastly, he did not know fear, and had no feeling of terror. It was most difficult to over-awe this unprepared pagan.
His sense of equality became most marked, the light in
his grey eyes shone most gaily and clearly, when he was
confronted with authority. He was a man who would be
impious enough to tear aside the veils of mystery and step
before the Eternal Throne in the imagined right of his
security as a man with an intelligence, and take his
chances. And this was the worst sign of all.

All these things were very baffling. With such a man it
was necessary to begin at the beginning. It was necessary
to work on his emotions. It was necessary to undermine his
confidence. So Padraic mac Alphurn was set to this task,
for it was admitted that he was best qualified in dealing
with this kind of man.

II

THE DEATH OF OSCAR

IT WAS WITH THIS LAUDABLE INTENTION that Padraic said to Oisin in a kind and not too obvious way:

"Oscar, your son, he was dear to you?"

Oisin looked at him with his eyes full of shadows and answered:

"It is not possible to say how dear he was to me. It is not possible to say how dear he was to all who knew him, but to his father he was most dear of all."

"On the field of Gabhra he fell?"

"On the field of Gabhra he fell."

"It was a field of ruin?"

"It was a field of destruction," Oisin mourned softly; "it was a field of death. Ochone, the field of Gabhra, where the ranks of the Fianna fell before the sickle of a very swift reaper, and where the spirits of the hills and of the woods, and the spirits of the glens and of the air, fled affrighted before the carnage. Ochone, the field of Gabhra, where the blood ran in streams between the hillocks of the dead, and Ben Edair looked down on the bloody tide the Liffey bore out to the sea. Ochone, the field of Gabhra, where the spears and the mighty swords, the shields and the swift-speeding darts, were strewn under the cover of night like the wreckage of a smithy. Ochone, the field of

Gabhra, where the groans of the sorely wounded, and the battle-chants and yells of defiance of the heroes that went to meet death, and the mourning and lamentation of many women, rose up through the dusk to meet the quiet stars. Ochone, the field of Gabhra, where the living strode alone through the carnage to find the faces that were dear to them, and the night was alive with torches that threw a mournful flame. Ochone, the field of Gabhra, where the eagles and the crows, and each sort of unclean bird, quarrelled for the flesh of the beautiful and the brave, though there was enough for all. . . ."

This deep-felt lamentation was now mounting in volume, and Padraic mac Alphurn was in some fear that it would put him astray out of his matter. So taking advantage of a moment when Oisin had to pause for breath, he said firmly and loudly, hoping to distract his attention:

"And did Oscar slay many men?"

Oisin looked at him with a glance of the utmost indignation and said:

"Is it Oscar? He went through the battle-hosts of Tara like a hawk through a flock of birds, or like a rock of thunder. Was he not our leader that day with the silken standard? He slew the lord of Munster, and he slew the lord of Connacht, and many a famous hero went down before him that day, till he met the other Oscar—Oscar mac Garraidh, the pure, the brave, the noble."

"How is this?" said Padraic. "Do you then praise your enemy, and the enemy of your son?"

Oisin looked at him in the extremest surprise. It was some time before he seemed to understand the question. Then he said:

"A worthy enemy, O bishop, is better than a treacherous friend. To contend with a brave man is better than to colloquy with a knave. It is a coward, uncertain of his own purpose, who will demean his enemy. It was not so we of the Fianna used our foes. By truth and the might of our hands we came safe out of every conflict; and there was mourning and wonder in our ranks when the pure Oscar mac Garraidh fell before the bright sword of my son, and there would have been mourning and wonder in the hosts of Tara if it had been his luck to prevail."

"There is only one kind of praise that is worthy," Iserninus said coldly, "and that is the praise of God over the enemies of righteousness."

"That is true, O cleric," Oisin remarked. "But as to that I would say two things. The first is that the enemies of righteousness are not all on one side or indeed the workers of righteousness. And the second is that I was brought to hear your singing this morning. It is not in bellowing that noble men find pleasure, but in poems of discriminating praise and in talking of the Fianna of Ireland."

Seachnall, at this, looked first at Iserninus, then at Auxilius, who sat silent, and then at Padraic. He had cleared his throat to speak, but now he decided to say nothing. For Padraic mac Alphurn was a man who, when he had decided to draw his aim on a mark, did not turn aside to regard other things. In that lay his authority. So he now said:

"Oscar died then?"

"It was so, he died. He hewed his way through the ranks of the living till he met Cairbre of the red spears, son of the monarch of Ireland. He bore the standard for Tara, and so it was silken standard for silken standard, bravery for bravery, purity for purity, and skill with skill. This Cairbre had no fear of battle, and was without dread before his enemy. And my son was Oscar. It was his valour that prevailed, but in that moment he fell also, and the two were dead together."

III

MORE OF THE DEATH OF OSCAR

MAC TAILL BROKE THE SILENCE after these sorrowful words by saying:

"So both standards fell. Ireland was left without armed men, and the monarch's son died. How often it is, O hero, that battles come to that end; that the purpose for which they are fought is undone in the fighting. The battles may be won, or they may not be won, but the standards are lost."

"I do not well understand you," said Oisin. "Is not the battle enough to itself?"

"I do not think so," Mac Taill said. "The value of the

battle is the worth of the standard, but if the standard is lost in the battle, then what is the worth of the battle? And it is often so among men, as I have seen. It is mostly the case that the standard is lost when the battle is won, and that is a great mystery; for it would seem that it is better to be defeated and to preserve the standard than to win and to lose the standard, and it would seem further that it is easier to remember the standard in defeat than to remember it in victory, and that is the greatest mystery of all."

"I do not agree with you at all," Oisin said. "It is best of all to win, but it is enough to fight; but it is only good to fight or to win when there is strength in the hand, truth on the lip and cleanliness in the heart. That was always our watchword, and the watchword in each man is the best standard of all. It was so we of the Fianna of Ireland used to think, whatever the cause we espoused."

"It is not so; I am sure it is not so," said Mac Taill. "It is the only disaster to lose the standard." And his glance for the briefest of moments fell on Iserninus before he plunged into the deepest of thought.

"The standard is nothing," said Oisin. "It is the only disaster to lose the good heart, and that was what Cairbre had, and Oscar my son."

This discussion continued no longer, for Mac Taill was still plunged in the deepest of thought; and Padraic mac Alphurn regarded him kindly and critically before he took the vacated place.

"They both died together so," he said.

"Cairbre fell first," Oisin answered with a little touch of rebuke, "and so it was my son got the victory. Then he fell too, wounded to death. There was not a spear's breadth from his hair to the soles of his feet that was whole, but his face only. His back was pierced by Cairbre's sharp spear. It was a swift and cunning navel-wound, and his entrails were severed in twain."

"You came to him, O hero, this son of yours that was so dear," said Padraic mac Alphurn, playing softly and carefully on his remembrance.

"I came to him," Oisin said. "When the carnage ceased I came and stood over him; and Caoilte came with me and stood over his six beautiful sons. I found my son lying there, lifted on his left elbow, his shield by his side. His right hand clutched his sword, and the blood poured out through his equipment.

"I laid the shaft of my spear on the ground, and I raised a cry over him. O bishop, I then bethought me what I should do after him.

"Oscar gazed up at me, and the sight was pain enough for me to bear. He extended his two arms towards me, endeavouring to rise to meet me. I grasped the hand of my son, and sat down by his left side. From the moment of my sitting by him I did not give any more heed to the world.

"Then my manly son said to me, and he at the end of his life, 'I return my thanks to the gods for thy safe escape,

O father.' I shall not tell a lie, I had no answer for him until Caoilte then came towards us to look at Oscar.

"So we remained till the coming of the next day, when we saw coming towards us through the slaughter the great Finn mac Cumhail, my father. We all saluted Finn, but he made no reply to us till he came where lay Oscar of the sharp weapons.

"The moment Oscar saw Finn directing his way towards him, he looked on the face of that prince and saluted his grandfather. He lifted his voice then, and said to the great son of Morna: 'I concede my head to death since I behold thee, O Finn, my leader.'

"Sad was the great Finn, and he said, 'O Oscar, good son of a good son, after you I shall be powerless, after you and after the Fianna of Ireland.' When he heard those mournful words his spirit darted out of Oscar. He stretched down both his arms and he closed his beauteous eye.

"Then we raised the manly Oscar aloft on the shafts of our spears, and we mourned for him till we buried him beside the field, together with Oscar mac Garraidh, the pure, the brave. Finn wept not for his own son, and he did not weep for his brother. He never shed tears for anyone on this earth. But he wept that day for Oscar."

When Oisin had finished his tale he was silent for a long while. And they were all silent, for it seemed a little thing to engage in speech after a tale so sorrowful. Then Oisin raised himself till he towered over his companions, and he said:

"I beg to be excused, O bishop, for my sorrow at this moment is very great."

IV

THE FIRST TRIAL OF OISIN

So GREAT WAS OISIN'S sorrow that when Brogan went in to see him later that day, and invite him to more colloquy with the bishops, he could not get across the distance with which Oisin had surrounded himself. It was not that Oisin did not answer him, but that he did not hear him, or see him, or otherwise perceive him, and not to be heard, seen or otherwise perceived, is all one with not being there at all. It is to be insulted by both Time and Space. The four walls of the one room stretched about the two of them, with a floor beneath and a roof above, but Brogan felt that he and this silent, huge figure beside him were not on the same plane of space, or in the same part of time; and he was—not angry—but mortified, deeply mortified. Strictly speaking, it is to be mortified not to be on the same plane of space or part of time that one thinks one is, or wishes to be. And all these metaphysical puzzles were stirred up in Brogan's brain as he went back to the bishops, simply by the failure to get an answer out of Oisin.

So great was Oisin's sorrow that when Soichell went in to him with his supper, even he failed to lift him out of

the dark waters in which he was sunk. It was not that
Oisin by this silence implied any criticism, at that moment, of the supper, although it had gone back to the
severe and spiritual regimen of wheywater and stirabout.
Auxilius, who by his energy took the lead in such bodily
matters, had decided that, though fasting as a virtue and
a privilege was wasted on Oisin, it would have a good,
because unsettling, effect on his emotions, and so help to
overcome the historical disadvantage that weighed against
him. But the wisdom was wasted. It is doubtful whether
another supper the same as the last would have roused
Oisin. It is only known for certain that gruel failed, and
had to be taken away again by Soichell, in spite of its
spiritual properties.

For, coming upon his bliss of over two hundred years,
Oisin's loss was as though it had only occurred the day
before. This is not surprising. These long spaces of time
are only encountered in the history of nations; and that
history proves, that events only begin to be recent when
they have happened an hundred years before.

Even when he began, with powerful grimaces, to eat his
spiritual food the following day, he still did not take any
notice of his fellowmen beyond directing glances of in-
creasing hostility at Soichell. Iserninus and Auxilius were
troubled because of this. It seemed to them pure waste of
a splendid mood most apt for the breeding of repentance,
like throwing away the divine culture for the breeding of
the germ in which they practised. A moment such as this

might never recur. They might be charged with the responsibility. So they came themselves to see him. They addressed him in tones shrewd and compelling. They expostulated with him. But he did not heed them. Perhaps he did not even hear them.

Never had they seen so terrific a sorrow, for they were not accustomed to the heroic. It appealed to them as specialists in rare moods of anguish. Yet, here was a perfect thing being lost just by reason of its sheer perfection. It was a terrible thing for them to contemplate. Yet Oisin did not even mind them.

Oisin was alone with the memory of a love, and that was a better thing for him, apparently, than to be concerned with a present troublesome world. Oscar dead, it would seem, was more to him than Iserninus living. Strange, yet so it appeared. For he drank his gruel and he drank his wheywater, and the convulsing grimaces he made were his only acknowledgement of the world to which his body had returned. For many days these were his only acknowledgement, while he sat on his bed surrounded by distance and enveloped in sorrow. For many days these grimaces were his only spasms of pain, that is to say, of life.

It was they who brought him back to life by reminding him of his body. Nothing will more surely bring a man back to mortality than poor victuals or fasting, for nothing will more quickly make him aware of his body. The same is true, to a lesser extent, of women. Especially it is true of heroes, whose splendid daring and enterprise are built up

on copious meals. Copious meals, with heroes, are not a sur-
render to the flesh, but an alternative part and necessary
groundwork of the fierce zest that constitutes their herodom. Fires that consume cannot blaze and flash without
fuel. And even the fires of sorrow are limited in that
way, too.

The signs of Oisin's return were that his grimaces grew
more and more powerful, and more and more convulsive.
On the fourth day he rose up with a roar, and snatched the
bowl of stirabout out of Soichell's hands, and clapped it
over Soichell's lean pate, so that the contents ran down his
sparse and frugal beard. Then he seized the horn of whey-
water and dashed it down his back inside his hair-shirt.
Then he lifted his foot gently to propel Soichell outside
the door. At least, he intended to do this, but in fact he
lifted his foot so hastily, being unaccustomed to such short
distances, that Soichell was shot out into the hall at an
enormous speed that made him dizzy, and there collapsed,
and did not recover consciousness for twenty-four hours.

That night Oisin did without his supper, and the following day he returned to the company of the bishops.

V

THE TRIAL OF OISIN IS CONTINUED

BECAUSE OF SOICHELL being still without consciousness, Oisin was in a sore state the next morning.

None of the household would go near him, so that he was like to do without his breakfast as well as his supper. Heroes, however, as part of their training for herodom, in the old world when heroism was an active exercise, and not merely a negative reflection, were always ready for such situations. They preferred to be waited upon, and that was the human side of their characters, but it was nothing to them to wait upon themselves, and that was the heroic.

Consequently, when Oisin, by his bell-like thunderings, had only succeeded in terrifying the servants the more, without comfort to himself, he went forth to the kitchen in a spirit of self-help. Directly he appeared there, the servants dropped their pans and utensils of their skilled craft with a musical noise that sounded through the whole house and fled into the country, and did not return for two days.

This was most annoying to the bishops. In the first place it was annoying because they desired no noise of Oisin until they had first got him baptised and could exhibit him as a trophy of grace. In the second place it was annoying because it meant carrying fasting to its logical conclusion, and it is well known that when religion is carried to its logical conclusion it becomes no more religion but fanaticism, against which all teachers of true doctrine have inveighed.

For when the bishops (who always acted together) ran into the kitchen, after hearing the mellow and gong-like summons of the pans falling to the ground, they found that Oisin had already consumed the better part of their breakfast. And he looked at them with a dignity so compelling and proud that they found themselves unable to reprove him for what he had eaten, or to restrain him from what he had yet to eat. They had neither the satisfaction of their breakfast nor the satisfaction of moral grandeur. They were merely baffled and without episcopal resource.

Then it was that the powerful sanity of Padraic mac Alphurn rose to its height. He led the way back to the common hall, and addressed the company in these words:

"This is sent to us to compel us to accurate modes of thinking. For we see that though punishment may be endured vicariously, vicarious substitution is not equally potent in the matter of breakfast."

The shadow of a smile passed over his stern face as he looked for a moment at Iserninus, but Iserninus did not heed the saintly joke. He was thinking that they had missed the opportunity of Oisin's sorrow, and now they had missed the opportunity of his hunger. To miss two such opportunities was a great responsibility. It was not to be avoided by saintly flippancy. Time was passing by, and Oisin was restored to pagan robustness and good health, those signs of unpreparedness.

To Iserninus the loss of his breakfast was a little thing. It only heightened his exquisite fervour. More than that he would give if it were required of him. But the gain to Oisin of all their breakfasts was a spiritual calamity.

Master-general as he was, he had thought to encompass Oisin's salvation by destroying his reserves. But Oisin, by putting a distance about him, and by attacking the kitchen, had overcome these attacks in the most natural manner. He sighed. There was no alternative. He disliked the frontal attacks that Padraic mac Alphurn favoured. After all, the sending of Padraic to Ireland was a questionable affair, against which, at the time, he had protested. Padraic was crude; he was unlearned; he was human; he had no appreciation of the subtle and austere, besides being woefully lacking in theology. Yet, in an issue like this, with a pagan two hundred years out of date, he had his qualities. It was clear that the battle for Oisin's soul would have to be left to him.

"Since fasting is compelled on us," he said, "it was not for nothing. If it had been for nothing it would not have been at all. If we complain or are angry, then we lose an opportunity for virtue. It was predestined, but we may also exercise our free-will by resolving to abstain from breakfast. It is a great mystery, but so it is."

"It would be annoying but for that," Auxilius said. "So much energy is required for the work to be done, and man's days on this earth are few. Yet, prayer and fasting also are good works, even though one does not see much result from them."

At this moment Oisin came within the room and Seachnall was hindered from the original observation he was about to make. Oisin stood in the doorway looking on them and said:

"Prayer and fasting are two pursuits that I have never

followed. The Fianna of Ireland were a company that was plentiful in bread. There was bread with them for every mouth, for it was their opinion that they that were without strength were without power, and they that were without power were without virtue. Ochone, that I should be now a weakly old man without banquets and without feasts, without drink and without food, with my stomach that is sick after the stirabout of the clerics. My strength is gone, and gone my swiftness. The lack of victuals has left my body without power, and therefore I am without virtue. Dry-withered I am; sapless and fruitless I am: without beauty and energy. I cannot be virtuous, because there is nothing in me with which to be virtuous."

VI

THE CHALLENGE

ONE OF THE WISEST and most learned observers has remarked that the earth is strewn with evidences of man's progressive decline and degradation. These evidences betray themselves in the least suspected places. They crouch in corners, waiting to leap on the inattentive mind—or avoid regard in the bold and comely beauty of ancient statuary or picture.

So it was with Padraic mac Alphurn. As he looked at Oisin, framed in the doorway mourning his departed splendour, one of these evidences was revealed before him, and left indelibly on his mind an impression of the most unpleasant sort.

For the doorway, he noticed, perfectly framed the hero. Its width was in exquisite proportion to its height. The roof was in the like proportion; and the breadth and length of the hall were in the same delicate balancing of parts together. All were in perfect proportion. Hall and roof were parts of one whole with the doorway, and consequently, as Padraic mac Alphurn perceived, they were parts of one whole with the hero whom the doorway so admirably framed. For him the house might have been built. For him, indeed, it had been built. Since his day, over two hundred years before, Mankind had dwindled and diminished to their present littleness; but the builders of houses had gone on building the only kind they knew with a craftsmanship that had forgotten its association.

To say that Padraic mac Alphurn was disquieted would be to say a little thing. He was startled. It would not be too much to say that he was appalled. He felt the house weighing on him like a huge structure for which he was not fitted, as though he had by mischance wandered into a deserted temple of antique and colossal rites.

But Padraic was one of those rare men who the more startled they feel the more instant they are in attack. Had he not been of that sort he would never had thought of his present mission of recasting an old civilisation. He looked resolutely at Oisin. He noticed particularly the sinuous whorls of the embroidery of his tunic that, having wandered endlessly, returned upon their beginning. His eyes fell to the long bony shanks of his legs, and lifted to the long white beard and hair, now already a little yellow with age upon age, and finally to the grey eyes that looked on him with a direct and fearless glance. His own grey eyes kindled in response. In his breast a battle ardour flamed. The muscles of his jaws tightened firmly. Being, however, filled with the utmost determination he spoke with the utmost gentleness.

"You mistake, O hero," he said, "for it is not by his body that man is distinguished. His body is a little thing. Rightly considered, it is even a ridiculous thing, with some men more ridiculous than with other men. In the doctrine that I will teach you it is said that the One Only and True God, Who is also Three Persons, made man in His own Image; but it was not in respect of his body that this was said, for God is a Spirit and they that worship Him must worship in spirit and in truth, but in respect of his spirit. However well the body is fed, man will never be strong as a horse or as swift as a hound or as flighty as an eagle. He will never look as wise as an owl nor will he stand shapely as a stag. For bounds have been set to the possibilities of his body, and man is at the end of those possibilities. He may even decline from them, and more victuals will not restore him. To eat copiously, therefore, is a waste of energy that might be more profitably engaged. It is better to make more distinguished his distinction than to make more obvious his imperfection. Therefore in

the religion we have come to teach, man will become more
and more a spirit and less and less a body. The round belly
will be a disgrace and unnecessary flesh a shame. Men
will decline in body and advance in spirit, for only by so
doing can they escape the limits of this world into the
limitless freedom of the next."

For a swift second a look of extreme surprise passed
across Oisin's face at hearing himself addressed in these
remarkable but, to him, unusual words. But instantly it
resumed its heroic composure, and when Padraic mac
Alphurn finished on an eloquent period, Oisin at once
replied. He spoke severely, and he spoke as though the
subject were a familiar one to him.

"It is often the case," he said, "that words of the pro-
foundest wisdom from one wise man will sound to another,
equally wise, like wind in the eaves of a house. It is unaccountable that this should be so; but only what is unaccountable is significant. It is, no doubt, true that to
explain a mystery is to empty an ewer of wine, for an
empty ewer is of no interest to anybody. Otherwise I
should want to know why the spirit of man should be
housed in his body except for its profitable entertainment
there. I have seen bodies in which the entertainment would
not be profitable at all, O bishop. In that case the spirit of
man must suffer, it seems to me, for there must be some
proportion, based on experience, between the spirit and the
body. It must be so. It was not by his body but by his
spirit that my beautiful Oscar lifted a battle to victory on

his hands, but it could not have been done without a body that matched the spirit, and such a body must be nourished and practised. Ochone, my beautiful Oscar, who left me in sorrow and the world in loss; it is not much your spirit could accomplish, for it is a lean entertainment it would receive in the body of a hungry mannikin, the like of which is all I now can see."

Mac Taill had looked at Padraic mac Alphurn, and he now looked at Oisin, with eyes that would tear their meanings from each of them; but they were, each of them, so occupied with the other that neither of them gave any heed to him. For Padraic mac Alphurn turned to face his opponent, and said in a tone of the firmest possible gentleness:

"The man that is well-nourished in his body is sluggish in his mind and weak of spirit, O hero. That is so."

And Oisin answered as resolutely:

"The man that is not well-nourished in his body is always thinking of that body, and therefore has no thought at all, O bishop, but only a peevish tearing asunder of motives. He has no spirit, for the spirit is most perfect when it shines in action like a devouring flame, perceiving all things, knowing all things, possessing all things, unaware of itself, not when it gnaws at right and wrong like a hungry mongrel at a bone. That is likewise so, O bishop."

"The spirit of man and the thought of man rise as the body drops away," Padraic mac Alphurn said, still more gently and firmly.

"The spirit of man, and the thought of man, cannot rise until the body is first nourished," Oisin said, still more resolutely and courteously.

"The wisest man who ever lived," Padraic said, with a kindly smile of conviction, "fasted and prayed all night on a mountain. That was for an example to us, O hero."

"It was a good example," Oisin said with an equal smile of courtesy, "for it is well known that mountains are inhabited by the *Sidhe*, great of power and beauty, who issue at night. And how may one climb a mountain until one is first nourished?"

The faintest of colour flushed Padraic's austere cheeks as he answered:

"Your ignorance of true doctrine, O hero, has snared you into a most evil perversion. He went to commune with His Father, the One Only and True God."

"That is right, too," Oisin said. "The *Sidhe*, are they not the beautiful company in the courts of God?"

"Not so, not so. The *Sidhe* are the wicked spirits of earth. God is the God of Heaven."

"The portals of earth are the gates of Heaven."

Oisin spoke these words with a simple gesture of dignity, like one conscious of inventing a saying that, like all sayings of doubtful meaning, was to become for ever famous. But, like other sayings destined to become famous, it aroused an immediate hubbub of contradiction.

"O impious man," said Iserninus, "do you not know that this world will be burned in flames while God, attended by His chosen few, rides in triumph over the furnace?"

"Indeed, that is most true," said Seachnall. "And I, even I, shall be present on that occasion, though I am the most unworthy of the chosen."

"Impious and ignorant man," said Auxilius. "This earth is to be subdued. In order that it may be subdued it must be organised. The strength for that comes only from heaven."

"I wonder," said Mac Taill and stopped. "It is just possible," he added, and stopped again.

But Padraic mac Alphurn cut the clamour short with one word.

"Mudebroth," he said. He looked around him with a flash of authority in his eye like the flash of a grey sword in the hand of a practised swordsman, and there was silence. Then he looked up at Oisin still standing in the framework of the doorway proportioned by the roof and the walls, and the length and breadth of the hall, and his authority trembled before the picture of man's decline. The thin-drawn sound of two centuries of man shrinking and shrinking came stilly to his heart across an infinity of distance, and to quell that sound he lifted his voice.

"O Oisin," he said, "you speak in ignorance, because you do not know. Therefore you are forgiven. I will give you knowledge, and then you cannot be forgiven."

"Is it better to know, or is it better to be forgiven, which?" asked Oisin of his soul.

"Man must always know, because for that he was born.

I will tell you, therefore, of the wisest man who ever lived, and He was wisest because He was also God."

"Finn mac Cumhal was the wisest man who ever lived, and he is now with the gods. When he desired wisdom he bit his thumb through the flesh to the bone, and through the bone to the marrow, and through the marrow to the nerve, and then he had wisdom. It was wisdom, indeed, because the blood flowed with it. He taught that whatever happened was best. It was a good faith for warriors to believe, but if he had returned after two hundred years he might not have taught it. It was, no doubt, the same with your champion, O bishop, for none can control the future."

"I will match my champion against Finn mac Cumhal," said Padraic mac Alphurn.

"I will match Finn mac Cumhal against any man for all that a man may be," said Oisin.

VII

THE FORGIVENESS OF SOICHELL

So IT WAS AGREED. The contest was set for the morrow, and Oisin and Padraic withdrew from one another to reflect apart on the virtues and images of their champions. For Oisin's part the reflection filled him with melancholy. When he brought before his mind the picture of the great commander of the Fianna at the hunt, in the battle, in council, at the feast, slender and beautiful and wise, he mourned a past world when men acted because they knew, and he mourned his return to a world when men knew before they acted, and often knew and did not act.

He mourned a world when knowledge was as careless as the sight of the eyes; and he mourned a world where knowledge was a troubled labour of the brain.

At this fruitless reflection he was engaged when Soichell entered with his supper. And Soichell set his supper down before he spoke. Then he said:

"I forgive you, O Oisin, for lifting your foot against me."

Oisin regarded him for some time severely before replying:

"The Fianna never told untruth, and falsehood was never imputed to them."

This seemed to puzzle Soichell, so that he said:

"I do not very well understand you, O Oisin."

"I say this," Oisin said, "because it seems to me that you do not forgive me at all. If you did, you would act as if that little scene had never occurred. Instead of this, you come to be revenged on me by seeking to assert a superiority over me. To say that you forgive me is to exult over me, and to exult over me is to be revenged on me. And I will not allow that. I will not permit myself to be debased by your humility. I will not be enslaved by your meekness. I reject your forgiveness, O miserable dispenser of food that my belly scorns. I will assert my right, and I will prove yours, by doing to you again——"

He rose as he said this; but Soichell did not wait. He left the room hastily, firmly convinced that extreme age had affected Oisin's morals, and probably his sanity also.

TRUE Forgiveness

THE FOURTH BOOK

I

PREPARATIONS FOR THE ASSEMBLY

Stupendous were the preparations for the assembly in which the contest was to be decided. Except Oisin, who at once discarded reflections that only made him melancholy, all the others of the household, from Padraic mac Alphurn down to the lowliest servant who came traipsing back from the surrounding villages and woods, spent all that day and all that night in agonies of meditation, that is to say of concentration. They were able to do this with all the greater potency, there being nothing else to do in the absence of the regular meals of the day. Without that familiar framework they had not the support of custom, and so they meditated, and meditated in agony.

That is not to say that any of them did anything other than as he always did when he got the opportunity to serve his own inclination. Not at all. By no means. It was not possible. Men are strangely and mysteriously made, and it is a commonplace to observe that women are still more strangely and mysteriously made. They are what they are, and they are what they were born, together with what their experience has made them. They are a bundle of memories, young and old, earthly and unearthly. Their pasts are before them, and it may be said that they advance into the future posterior forward. For if it is true that their past is the prophecy and augury of their future, as is most clearly the case, seeing that the future can only be the unpredicated outcome of the momentous past, then it is equally true that in facing the future they are only facing their past, and that in experiencing the past they were only defining their future.

To be sure, all these things are great mysteries. But no matter, that does not make them any the less true. Truth is itself the greatest mystery of all. Men have been searching for truth ever since they invaded the earth, and though each generation of them has flung its cap in the air, and held the hidden treasure proudly in the hollow of its hand, each succeeding generation has mocked at it and done the same with some other discovery. So much for discoveries, and so great a mystery is truth.

This much is, if not true, at least undeniable, that men are what they are and that they cannot be anything else. It is the great fact established for all time by Oisin in his first conversation with Padraic. When they are liberated from the custom that perverts them, and when they are loosened from the framework that shuts them in, they simply with gladsome hearts become stupendously themselves

—they simply are, and that is a stupendous thing. Meditation is such a liberation, such a loosening, especially when those pivots of life, the meal-hours of the day, can no longer be relied on. Consequently each man of the household did that thing, and occupied himself with those thoughts, that most perfectly expressed that urge-forward into the future—that prow of his soul's ship which cleaves the waters of the boundless ocean of Time—which we call his inclination.

I I

THE PREPARATIONS ARE CONTINUED

LUACHRA MAC LONAN, for example, was persuaded to go into the closet of his own room, and to pray —to pray for Oisin's soul that it might be mysteriously saved by the Wisdom of the Ages. No question about it, he went to his room; and no question about it, he repeated the one or two phrases that expressed that modest request till he got utterly tired of them, and till it was clear to him that they meant what they had begun by meaning—nothing at all. Then he began to muse and to meditate. The eyes of his soul began to see visions, for it is by the vision we perceive that which is, and it is by the brain we think that which is not. He saw with unimaginable delight the figure of a splendid warrior, vigorous beyond compare, not particularly beautiful (for beauty is, as it is said, only skin-deep), but with that compelling masterfulness stamped on his features that may be likened to ugliness, but is no more ugly because it expresses a mind so forceful that it holds the will of all the world in its sway. He saw that figure stand before him with beetling brows, pursed lips and thunderous eyes. He saw huge muscles burst that frame into lumps and contortions, standing on its arms like knots and ropes of wrought steel, and yet without marring the prodigious symmetry of the whole. He saw it hold an armful of spears in one hand and a mighty battle-axe in the other, while a shield of terrific circumference hung carelessly over the shoulder.

After surveying this figure delightedly for some time, he felt that he must run and tell Oisin about it. In the morning would be too late. This was the conception to save a man's soul, and everything else about a man. But he did not know that what he had seen was the Luachra mac Lonan of his dreams.

For his part, Iserninus prayed all the time. Never once did his lips cease to repeat the words he had learned by rote, and so thoroughly mastered that it was no trouble to him to continue them for ever. He fingered his beads, and a constant buzz sounded from his mouth like a hive of swarming bees. The pace of his prayers never changed, the words following one another at swift and regular intervals of time that never varied by the minutest fraction of a second.

It was thus he prayed for Oisin's soul. But having by these means subdued his other activities, having drawn off his other activities into that constant iteration, he too began to see visions. He saw a Great White Throne. The whiteness was not soft and fluent and comely. It dazzled and hurt. It was hard and assailing. It asserted itself, and was rigorous and compelling. It was a whiteness that excluded every other colour, not the whiteness that includes and suggests every other colour. It was a whiteness that might as well have been blackness for all the good its whiteness did for it, or for anybody else.

On this Great White Throne sat a Great White Figure. The one whiteness was like the other whiteness. There was no difference. This Figure had in its hand an episcopal crook and on its head an episcopal crown. It had a pale, austere face with faint and cold blue eyes. It had thin lips and a lofty, narrow brow. Much severity had made its face, that might otherwise have been benignant, seem cruel and crafty and logical. It was a face of blighted beauty.

Before that Great White Figure on the Great White Throne, alone across the infinite expanse of the Great White Pavement beneath the three steps of the throne, came a human figure in withered and faded clothes. This was Oisin. Only now it was the figure on the throne that was huge and lofty, and Oisin who crept across the great pavement like an ant.

He saw the Great White Figure regard Oisin with cold, contemptuous eyes, and then indicate him with outstretched forefinger. Then he saw other smaller and subservient white figures come into being and seize Oisin and hurl him over the edge of a cloud, hurtling into space with a clatter of weapons. He saw him fly through space, all legs and all arms, into a lake of fire, whose flames leapt up to receive him, lick him and engulf him. And he heard through infinity a thin, desolate cry of agony.

As Iserninus knelt and saw and heard these things, his prayers went just a shade faster, such was his fervency. He approved of them all. His mind affirmed that God was just even while his lips repeated his prayers by rote. But he did not know that it was not God whom he had seen in a vision, but the Bishop Iserninus of his own dreams.

III

MORE PREPARATIONS

EACH IN HIS OWN CHAMBER, the others were similarly engaged. All day and all night they all prayed. They all prayed for the one thing, and they all prayed in the same form of words, but each man of them all had a vision distinct and separate from the vision of any other.

As has been said, even the servants prayed, for, the menial tasks being set aside to which Eternal Wisdom had appointed them, in the matter of prayers they were the same and as potent as any other. Some of them saw Oisin in heaven, and they with him hunting and fighting and leaping in a freedom as spacious as space, where meals cooked themselves and floors swept themsleves, where one

man was as good as another, and some men better than
most, though they had been servants once before. Others
saw themselves in heaven, hunting Oisin out of it as he
had hunted them out of the kitchen. For most of them the
conspicuous beauty of heaven was that Soichell was not
in it, it having been decided that he was only fit for the
other place, because while on earth he had set himself up
for being better than another man, with his harsh rules and
silent upstartishness.

Seachnall prayed with a fervency that was feverish. He
had the greatest difficulty in bringing his powers to the
point of meditation. This was because his mind was troubled. He was not sure whether he ought to write another
hymn in praise of Padraic, or whether he ought to offset
that first hymn by writing one in praise of Iserninus. If he
could only be sure it would be easier for him to meditate,
for his meditation would necessarily be influenced by the
knowledge which of these two would come uppermost in
the end.

Therefore his meditation was confused and impotent.
It was as impotent as a river that runs into a number of
little streams. And therefore his prayers were at times a
mere gabble while at other times they were as sluggish as
a summer stream—quite unlike the swift and punctual
amble of the prayers of his brother Iserninus.

Auxilius prayed. He did not pray so fast as Iserninus
nor so unsteadily as Seachnall. The speed of his prayers

was uniform though it was not rapid. Being uniform, they subdued at length his other activities, and drew them off into their constant iteration, enabling him to meditate and to concentrate and to see visions. His vision came slowly to him, not merely because his other faculties were tougher and not so easily subdued, but also because the vision itself was solid and complex.

In his vision, he, too, saw a throne, but it was not a Great White Throne. It was solidly built of earthly gold on a pedestal of costly marble. It was encrusted with precious stones, and on the pointed arch to which it mounted a wondrous diadem of three crowns was fashioned in diamonds that caught the light from every angle. It was a wonderful throne. It was so costly as to be worth, not the ransom of one empire, but the ransom of many empires.

He saw this throne set within a building into which the light struggled through pictured windows of richly coloured glass, arriving dim and mysterious and subdued. The dome of this building was so vast that it filled his mind with delight and awe. The light elsewhere faded into a richly patterned gloom, and little else of the interior could be seen.

One sat in that throne who was not a Being but a Man. The costliness of throne and dome was but a thing for scorn except as symbol of That Man's power and the power which That Man represented. Far outside the dusky building fell a circle of sunlight on green sward and woods

that swayed with the wind. In that sunlight stood Another Man. This was Oisin. He was dressed in old and
faded clothes; he was himself old and faded, but he stood
in his individual strength and defied That Man. But That
Man lifted his finger, and the building organised itself
against the green sward and swaying woods, so that Oisin
gasped for air, and could not breathe, and finally sub-
mitted his will and soul into the keeping of That Man.
Then the steady normal course of the prayers of Auxilius
blared forth like a trumpet, and his bowels were wondrous
full of compassion and love, but whether for Oisin or for
That Man and his Throne it is not right to enquire.

The trumpet-tone was heard by Soichell in the next
room, but Soichell did not mind it. He found prayer an
infinitely blessed thing, in part owing to the fact that it
was so much more comfortable to kneel than to sit. So
beautiful was the vision that filled his reflective soul that
his prayers stumbled along, broken of wind and halting
of gait. He saw a Being of very saintly appearance. This
Being was bearded, but this beard was not coarse and
abundant, but sparse and spiritual. This Being was exces-
sively thin, of face and of frame, as all high spiritual
beauty is thin to excess. Beneath this Being knelt a man
in old and faded garments, humbly asking forgiveness.
This man was Oisin. And the Being lifted a hand over
Oisin and gladly forgave him all his sins, though they were
many. And Soichell was very glad.

I V

THE PREPARATIONS ARE CONCLUDED

THE LONG DAY and the long night drew at length
to a close. And as the long day and the long night drew to
a close, the prayers, that Oisin's soul might be saved by
the Wisdom of the Ages, drew to their close even also.

Such a volume and such a fervour of praying for one
man had never been known before. At least, there is no
record of the like in all the precious books. It stands alone
beyond the power of skill to do it justice. This is not surprising, as there never had been a case before, and there
has not been a case since, of a man coming back to earth
over two hundred years in Tir-na-nOg, and that man a
hero, one of the Fianna of Ireland.

This thought it was that perplexed Mac Taill, and
brought all his prayers to confusion. He found himself, in
a glad and defiant voice, repeating poems that he distinctly
knew to be pagan of origin, even while he thought that he
was saying Christian prayers. And not only did he confuse
the pagan and the Christian eras, but he found himself
also confusing the Cuchulain Cycle with the Fenian Cycle,
which was only in a lesser degree as bad. For this poem
was a poem in praise of the peerless bravery of him who
warred while Christ taught on earth.

These things distressed Mac Taill. He tortured himself.

He began to doubt his own election. In pain and agony of mind he brought himself to steady meditation by a great effort of his will. He saw a big bearded man, with misty troubled eyes, standing by the shores of a lake, which was the lake of Galilee. This man was burly and powerful of frame, but shy and gentle of manner. He was sunk in the deepest possible reflection, for had he not, though inarticulate of thought, undertaken to right all wrong and cure all suffering in a world where he saw nothing but wrongs to be righted and sufferings to be cured? Then he saw another man dressed in clothes that were old and faded, but quaint and strangely becoming. This other man went up to the first and gave him the sword that was in his hand, and received it back from him again. The two then went out to war against giants in their dens, and to fight all monsters by the way, and to be such heroes as heroes never were before in all the world.

Then the tears flowed down Mac Taill's burly, bearded face out of his misty troubled eyes, for he perceived that he had not only confused the pagan and the Christian eras, and the Cuchulain Cycle with the Fenian Cycle, but that he had also confused Ireland with Palestine. He was tormented. He beat his hands on his breast. He began to pray, not for Oisin but for himself. And he would have been deeply surprised if anyone had told him that in so doing he was praying for Oisin in the best of possible ways.

There was no such doubt with Padriac mac Alphurn. He knelt unsupported in the centre of his bare room with his hands clasped before him like a man accustomed to lengthy praying. He prayed sometimes in Latin, but as that was bad, he prayed also in Gaelic, and that was worse. The indifference of his grammar, however, was no indication of confusion in his meaning, for his mind was clear as sunlight and his will steady as a well-tempered sword.

His words came firmly and punctually in order one after another, but they did not subdue his other activities, because his other activities had already been subdued, and they did not draw them off into any constant iteration; in the first place because there was no constant iteration, and in the second place because they had already been drawn into a purpose more constant than any iteration could possibly have been. He heard voices urging him to be spent in service; but he heard with waking ears. He saw a vision, but he saw with waking eyes. The vision was no new thing to him. Himself and his vision could not be distinguished apart, asleep or awake, by night or by day, for he was his vision, and his vision was he, both having been well matured together.

The vision he saw was of the sun bursting the clouds, cleaving the darkness with swords of light, and bringing wakeful energy to men who were tortured with temptation in sleep. As the sun broke the clouds, and lifted its countenance on the earth, it took the form of a Being, not young like a mere pagan god, but experienced and wise, with a long flowing beard, grey eyes and lofty brow. With his coming, heaven came to earth, and earth was lifted to heaven.

Leaping up from sleep he saw a man who brought a smile of joy, which was also a smile of conquest, to the Being who strode towards him. This man was dressed in somewhat faded clothes, but he was clearly a hero, and it was easy to see from the smile on the face of that Being that it loved heroes. Other heroes lay about him, still sleeping, and Padriac divined the purpose of the Being to waken those heroes, for he judged that it could not tolerate the thought of anyone sleeping once the sun had burst the clouds.

As Padraic mac Alphurn saw this vision the same sort of smile came over his face also. He thought of Oisin, and of Oisin's soul. His thoughts went to Finn mac Cumhal and to Caoilte mac Ronan, and to their souls, and to all the Fianna of Ireland and their souls. These were also heroes. Then he thought of the hero whom he served, and the smile deepened on his face. It was a smile of joy; it was also a smile of conquest, for it was impossible for him to think of any task in which he would not succeed.

Even as he smiled, his face was lit by the light of dawn. He took this as of good omen, for he always took everything that happened as of good omen, being somewhat disposed to the acceptance of good omens. And he rose up on his two feet. For the day of action had opened, and the best omen of all is the readiness for action.

V

THE ASSEMBLY IS SET

THE ONLY PERSON in the household whom all this pother touched lightly, yet touched deeply, and then touched not at all, was he about whom it circled. This was Oisin. Urged by Padriac mac Alphurn to meditate on Finn mac Cumhal, and to summon all his virtues and potencies before his thought, he had attempted to do so. But he found the virtues too few, the number of possible virtues being limited in nature, and the potencies too many, they being as frequent as the hours of their occasion.

So he thought simply of Finn mac Cumhal, whom he loved; and this made him very sad and very melancholy. He was sad because he desired to be able to put his hand in Finn's and serve him again. He was melancholy because he perceived a world in which such as Finn could not have lived, or which, living, he could have endured.

Therefore he slept. It seemed to him the only thing to do in such a world. He had heard Soichell say, in answer to a question of his, that he wished he could spend all day and all night in prayer, so to escape from temptation. He gathered that to be the ideal of life for this strange world to which he had so unluckily returned. It perplexed him greatly; yet to sleep outright seemed to him a quicker road to the same end; and so he slept sweetly while all the others prayed.

He was wrong. It was not the same thing. For he was refreshed the next morning when all the others were tired and sleepy.

That was plain to be seen in his face when they were all assembled. He was about a hundred and fifty years older than Seachnall, the next oldest of the assembly; but in fact he looked about a hundred and fifty years younger. And he and Padraic mac Alphurn were the only members of the assembly who showed no trace of nervousness.

"O Oisin," said Padraic mac Alphurn, "O hero of matchless fame, undoubtedly you have lived long. That you may die blessed. That you may walk the streets of the New Jerusalem striking a sweet harp and chanting a sweet hymn."

"That the same fate may also be reserved for you," said Oisin, hiding by his grave courtesy the fact that he did not know at all to what Padraic mac Alphurn was referring.

"We are come," continued Padraic, "to pit our lords against each other. But before that can be done we must have level ground on which to set them. We must agree in the matter of their comparison."

"It is not possible to compare men," said Oisin carelessly, "except in respect of their deeds."

"And also," added Padraic, "in respect of their words."

"It is the same thing," said Oisin. "It was the rule amongst the Fianna of Ireland that we did what we said, and what we said we did. The wisdom of the lips was only wise when it was the habit of the life. Otherwise it is only words, and words alone are the folly of weak and timorous men. For if what is said cannot be done, then it is waste of time to say it. It is better to eat and to drink, O bishop, than to spin idle fancies. It is better to sleep in the sun or to look on the fair hills of Ireland."

"True," said Mac Taill, with moving energy. "At least, I am sure it must be so. But what of the consequences? What of the consequences, O Oisin?"

"The consequences," said Oisin, with the same carelessness, "are not the concern of proper men. They are the snares of crafty men. It is the man of guile who speaks in council of consequences. I will not consent to compare Finn mac Cumhal, of the race of Baoiscne, with any man except in respect of his deeds."

"One could not make a society on those terms," Auxilius interrupted sharply. "It would come to ruin if it were insisted that men should put into act all the great things that we agree to be necessary, and especially those things that we agree to be beautiful. The beauty of truth is independent of mortal substance, and it is of mortal substance that societies are made, and it is by giving heed to mortal substance that we will persuade men to hold together. It is to profane truth to make it the measure of men's weakness, and it is to be unwise towards men also, when they have once professed the true faith, for otherwise we may lose them altogether, to the peril of their souls and to the loss of the Church. Consequently, it seems to me it is indispensable that we adhere to the beauty of truth, on the one hand, but be wise with mortal substance on the other hand. Does not the Scripture say that we must not let the right hand know what the left hand doth? And does it not also exhort us to be wise as serpents while being innocent as doves?"

Auxilius could have continued the whole of that day on this theme; and there is no reason to doubt that he would have done so but for the curious red fire he saw gathering in Padraic mac Alphurn's grey eye.

"I agree with Oisin," Padraic said, with the air of a man whom it would not take much to make truly angry. "I agree with Oisin," he added, in case he had been misunderstood. "Whatever is true to say is right to do, and if to do what is true succeeds in bringing the world down in ruin, will not the world be burned in fire at the last day for the same cause, O sister's son that is my brother in the Lord? What matter when it is burned so long as the truth is done? For be assured that truth will survive all ruin, and out of truth alone a new heaven and a new earth will be made."

Having with these words eased the anger that had been gathering in him, he turned to Oisin and said:

"The Lord whom I serve said many wise words, and for that I admire Him. But all that He said Himself did; and for that I love Him. It was the same with Finn mac Cumhal?"

"Finn mac Cumhal," said Oisin, "said many wise things,

and he was most wise when he did what he said. His counsel was for peace and for war. In battle, said he, meddle not with a buffoon, for, said he, he is but a fool. Wise words, O bishop, for victory at long odds is a shame. And as for Finn, he meddled not with fools, but kept his sword for the worthy."

"And what does that mean?" asked Auxilius, his bushy brows gathered in a frown across his wide forehead, and a flush brightening his face at the point of his high cheek-bones.

"It means what it means," said Oisin, and he looked at Auxilius with so cold an eye, and with so strange a meaning in that cold eye, that Auxilius was at once restored to a mind of Christian love.

VI
THE VIRTUES OF FINN

"AND WHAT WAS HIS COUNSEL FOR PEACE? Tell me that," said Padraic then.

"It was," said Oisin, "manifold, because peace is folded into many shapes, and war is unfolded into one straight issue. It was chiefly contained in this, that two-thirds of men's gentleness should be given to women and to little children and to the men of art who make poems, and that heroes should not be violent with the common people."

"Did he say that?" Padraic asked eagerly. "That was a good thing to say. I would be glad to say that."

"You could not say it," said Oisin, for there are neither women nor children in this house, and it is no proof to be gentle with them at a distance. It is only proof to be gentle when we desire peace from them in the house. For that sort, O bishop, become most beautiful when they are put up among the frosty stars.

"I will tell you how it is. When Finn, as I have told you, bit through his thumb to the nerve in the marrow of his bone, he became wise and could foretell the future. They were painful to do, both to bite the thumb in this way, and to foretell the future. But once when he did this he told us that a time would come when men would turn women into a dream and children to a vision of innocence. He said it would prove a most unfortunate thing for women and for children, that to happen, because it was a sign that they would be abused. He said it was part of the one cruelty to escape into a dream and to abuse the living. Better, said he, have woman for a comrade and listen to a poet's songs, than praise them for what they are not and be cruel to them for what they are. And that is how it was."

"It is clear to see," said Iserninus, "that this Finn mac Cumhal was of the school of cynics."

"What is a cynic?" Oisin asked in a ruffle of perplexity.

"A cynic," said Iserninus, severely, "is one who speaks in contempt of all the beautiful dreams and hopes that hold the heart of man unsullied amid the wreck of the years."

"How beautifully expressed," said Seachnall in an ecstasy. "Indeed, nothing could have been more exquisitely phrased."

"I am old," Oisin said, shaking his head in mournful wonder, "and do not understand the new trick of speech that men have adopted." And all the company looked upon the aged hero in infinite pity, he was so plainly out of date.

"And what else did he say?" Padraic mac Alphurn asked gently.

"If I were to stretch myself out into a lengthy tongue from here to distant Iorrus, and if you were one ear from this place to Loch Lein of beautiful shores, it would fail me to tell you a small part of the wisdom he spoke. For him to speak wisdom was as natural as for a rowan to grow berries—a matter of right place and fortunate inclination, not to be won with sweating. These things cannot be recalled, O bishop, because wisdom is a beautiful shaping of life. It lives in the spoken word.

"He told us to be true to all, for that was due to ourselves; to be gentle in the house, for that was due to our friends; to be surly in the pass, for that was due to our enemies; and to be in fear of none, for that was due to the gods. He told us also to accept all that happened as best, for that was due to our destiny; and to give back to every man full measure of his own giving, for that was due for his instruction in the goodness of good things and the badness of bad."

When Oisin had spoken these last words, all the bishops, except Padraic and Mac Taill, rose to their feet in various attitudes of horror. Iserninus' face seemed longer, and Auxilius' wider, and Seachnall's more shrunken. And with instant unanimity they all exclaimed with one voice:

"And what of forgiveness?"

Oisin seemed for a moment deafened by the clamour. Then he fixed his eye on Soichell and said:

"I never experienced it till yesterday. It is a terrible form of vengeance. I forgive you all the breakfast I had this morning."

In their indignation at this insult they all sat again and stared at him speechless, till Auxilius found voice:

"It was the same breakfast as we had," he said, "and what is good for one is good for all."

"Come, come," Padraic mac Alphurn remarked, stilling the uproar, "different people in different times say different things, but they all mean the same. My Master also was a great warrior," he said, bending his head reverentially. "Once, with no other weapon than a bit of a rope, he beat a hundred and one men flying in a heap from him. All legs and arms they were; and he whipped the hind part of them when he could, and when they sheltered the hind parts, he whipped other parts of them less suitable but serviceable enough. A hundred and one men, or thereabouts, and he with no more in his hand than a hank of rope."

"Ho," said Oisin, and his aged eye grew bright. "Ho," he said again. "That was a lusty deed. And what sort were these men?"

"They were merchants," Padraic mac Alphurn answered gravely.

"Merchants?" said Oisin. "What are merchants?"

"Merchants," Padraic answered, "are people who will neither let folk live nor worship God till they have first grown rich, and then they will not let them live or worship at all. Merchants are people who stretch their hand between the standing corn and the empty belly till they have first built a house with a different room to sleep in for each night of the year, and a different room to eat in for each day of the year. Merchants are people who stretch their faces between God and man till folk do not know which is God's face and which is the merchant's. They are very successful, are merchants. That is what makes them merchants."

"Let us not judge hastily," said Auxilius mildly. "There are good merchants and bad merchants. There are some who support the Church Militant, and will therefore rejoice in the Church Triumphant, and there are some who do nothing of the sort and will be destroyed in fire."

"Merchants," said Mac Taill, struggling to deliver himself of speech like a woman in labour. "Merchants." Then he composed himself and said quietly: "Being a bishop,

I cannot utter my opinion of merchants in fitting words."

"He drove them flying?" said Oisin.

"With a hank of rope," said Padraic mac Alphurn.

"That was good," said Oisin. "I would have given your Master service in such a battle, but not with a hank of rope. And Finn mac Cumhal would have given him service, though he was Captain of the Fianna of Ireland. For in the matter of gold, of silver, or concerning meat, Finn never denied any man. Nor, though another's generosity were such as might fit a chief, did Finn ever seek aught of him. If a man had only a head to eat with, and legs to travel on, Finn never refused him anything. Were but the brown leaf which the wood sheds from it gold, were but the white billow silver, Finn would have given it all away. If Finn had found but a merchant in Ireland that time he would have scattered his entrails through all the Tuaths for a warning. He would have purged Fodhla from her shame. He would have rescued Banba in her sorrow."

VII

EARTH AND HEAVEN

"THEY WERE BOTH GREAT WARRIORS," said Padraic mac Alphurn, going with that wary skill that long practice in the snaring of souls for his Master had taught him. No hunter ever trod so craftily. No question about it, no hunter ever looked so austere and untroubled. None of the others durst chide him for venturing so level a comparison, so grave he looked, so elderly innocent and casual.

But the high courtesy and perfect behaviour of the Fianna of Ireland in part saved Oisin from the snare that had been set for him. Lightly his glance touched Padriac mac Alphurn, falling like the dip of a sea-bird, before he looked away into the distance of his own thoughts and said:

"No doubt it is also creditable to whip merchants. And in the matter of comparison a hank of rope may certainly be called a weapon."

This saying of his is known for certain, because Brogan, the original authority for these debates, instantly recorded it as a model of classical reproof. It is to be found in his book. He also records that while he wrote Padraic mac Alphurn was silent, and this he notes as a sign of his appreciation.

Then Padraic spoke forthright, for his skill generally ended in impatience, as is the way with imperative men.

"A weapon is but a means," he said sharply. "The worth of a battle is the measure of the end that is gained."

"It is not necessary," Oisin remarked, "that a man be understood for him to be wise. And it is not necessary that a man be wise for him to be understood. But it is better for him to be both wise and understood. That is my judgment."

"What I mean is," urged Padraic mac Alphurn, "that greater battles may be won with a hank of rope than with

Finn's long sword, and the greatest battles may be won
without a weapon at all."

"I do not see," said Oisin, "how that can be. If one
were—— But no, I do not see it."

"It is of the battles of heaven I speak, not of the battles
of earth. The battles of heaven are fought in the spirit,
and the battles of earth are fought with the hands."

"Is it to fight in the spirit to fight with a hank of rope?
A hank of rope may serve a turn, but it is a demeaning toy.
It is not possible to make a poem about a hank of rope,
O bishop. Can you imagine such a thing?"

"I can, and do, O hero; for I have told you such a poem.
There is no better poem than the poem that chimes in
action, as yourself have said in requiring that we speak of
what men do and not of what men say. If there were no
beautiful things for men to do there would be no beautiful words for men to write; and one may destroy a soul
with a sword and save it with a hank of rope. That is
what I mean. For my Master came to save the souls of
men where your master only lived to destroy their beautiful bodies."

"That is not true," said Oisin. "For Finn mac Cumhal
was greatest, not when he slew men, but when he denied
himself to speak falsehood to them, and when he gathered them about his house and gave them all he had. But
he was also great when he slew valiant men, and it is
what they themselves would wish. For we must all die
sometime, and it is better to meet death by a brave man,

and with a ringing mind, than to draw up the knees in a bed."

Padraic mac Alphurn's mind suddenly sang out a happy music. He had drawn Oisin where he wished him. He drooped his eyes lest Oisin should see the light that was shining in them. He said:

"Greater when he saved than when he slew?"

"Saved?" Oisin pondered. "He saved nobody. He gave out of his own goodness. It was not possible for Finn to insult anybody with talking of saving them. Do you think Finn was a churl, a flat-foot, foul-sweating slave come to unmerited power, a red-eyed, wet-nosed, manner-less loon mistaken for a prince? Save? Is it not better to be honoured and slain than to be insulted and saved? Do you suggest that Finn——"

But Padraic intervened, for it was clear that Oisin was rapidly being consumed by his indignation.

"You mistake me, O hero," he said, and graciously bent to humour his pagan ignorance. "I am sure Finn would not insult anyone with his salvation. I meant that he was greater in his charity than——"

"Charity!" exclaimed Oisin, leaping to his feet as if the word had injured him, and raising his clenched hands over his head in a wild effort to control himself. "Did you say charity? Is it charity? Of all things charity? Finn, who thought nobly of all men because he thought nobly of himself, to be charitable. With these two hands I would strangle that word in your throat. Ochone, O Finn, that

I should hear this of you, who were always gentle and generous."

Padraic mac Alphurn was in desperation. The two centuries Oisin had missed in Tir-na-nOg seemed to put him beyond reach of the elevated conceptions to which men had risen since his day. Yet, he was stout of heart. He tried again, for it was his duty.

"I did not mean charity," he said. "What I meant was that he was greater when he was gentle than when he was fierce, greater in love than in the heat of battle."

"That is true," Oisin said. "Certainly that is true. But he was only gentle because his mind could also be fierce. Otherwise he would not have been gentle but feeble. I would have you know, O bishop, that Finn was not feeble, and that his love was a flame in his heart, not a thought in his mind."

Padraic's heart leapt up again in joy. There was much in this ancient pagan that he loved. He had a conviction that his Master would also have loved him, for it was impossible for him to think that his Master would have loved anyone whom he would not.

"That," said he in grave delight, "was his spiritual battle. That was his conquest over the flesh."

"What was his spiritual battle?" asked Oisin.

"To be consumed with love for men, to be gentle, to be generous, to be nobly-thoughted. For the flesh is sinful and utterly vile, and was ever tempting him to be otherwise. This is a great spiritual battle, O hero. It is the battle of all life."

"There was no battle," Oisin replied proudly. "Was he not Finn mac Cumhal, of the race of Baoiscne? Is there any temptation for a rowan to have other than red berries, or a sloe other than black berries, or for an oak to squat like a thorn, or for the blackbird of Leitreac Laoi to bray like an ass? It was his destiny to be as I say, and therefore he was Finn mac Cumhal. He was what he was —Finn mac Cumhal, that is to say. For no man can go outside his own skin, and no man can depart from his destiny."

"By the grace of God it is possible," said Padraic.

Oisin looked at him without understanding. Then his eye brightened, and gravely he shook his head.

"It is true," he said. "There is no controlling the gods. Once—it is a sorrowful tale—one of the gods turned Finn's mother's sister into a dog. But she could not help that, and so it was no fault for her."

"The One Only and True God, Who is also Three Persons in One, and whose poor servant I am," said Padraic, "can take a man who is a dog and make him into an angel bright as the sun. That is the good tidings I have to bear."

Padraic mac Alphurn trembled with the joy of what he was entrusted to deliver. But the effect on Oisin was mournful. He shook his aged head again till his beard quivered at the tips of the hairs long after he had ceased waving his chin.

"He could not help that either," he said, "and so it would be no virtue to him. There is no controlling the gods, one or three. But it is better to be oneself if one can. It is more satisfactory."

"It is better to be a bright angel than a dog," said Padraic mac Alphurn with the greatest severity of manner.

"It is better to be a free dog than an angel of necessity," said Oisin. "But it is best of all to be a man, if one may be such a man as Finn mac Cumhal was. And if one cannot be such a man it is good to follow him."

VIII

THE ENMITY OF THE GODS

PADRAIC MAC ALPHURN WAS IN DESPAIR. He was also distinctly irritated, for there is nothing so fretful as to seek a pathway through a forest and to meet obstruction at each point.

He could very easily have performed a miracle on the spot. He was in the mood for miracles. That part of the universal laws he encountered in Oisin's mind annoyed him, and he desired to over-ride them on the prancing steed of a miracle, if only to show that he was greater than they. He could, with a word, have turned Oisin into a porpoise or a pelican. He could have burned him in a flame, and opened the door to blow the ashes away. He could have cloven him in twain with an unseen sword and have interrupted for ever his casual blasphemies.

He could have done any of the miracles that are recorded to his skill in the unblemished annals of his works,
or have enriched his fame with some new and fantastic
miracle, to mark the singular mood of his mind. But he
did none of these things. The singular mood of his mind,
in fact, saved him, by restraining him. For singular moods
are also reflective moods, and this accompanying reflection revealed to Padraic that he rather respected the hero-
like extravagance of Oisin's wish for life.

He accepted this as a revelation of the spirit. Perhaps
he was right; perhaps that is what it was. But he was also
checked by other considerations. To destroy Oisin, or
turn him into a pelican, would be a highly unpopular act.
It was one thing to play these tricks with kings and druids
and other flunkeys of royalty or obsolete religion; it was
quite another to play them on a genuine hero just returned from Tir-na-nOg. With one they were a sign of
power; with the other a confession of defeat. So he accepted the revelation as a true one, and bent his will to
patience and to care.

To gain time while he thought, he said:

"Were there not times, O Oisin, O hero, when Finn did
that which was wrong, and was sinful?"

"There were not," Oisin answered. "We did not know
of such a thing as sin, and what we do not know we cannot experience."

"Sin is sin," said Iserninus suddenly and sharply, "and

is original. When Satan first fell from glory he sinned, and since then all have sinned. Finn mac Cumhal was born in sin, and lived and died in sin."

"It may be so," said Oisin. "But since he did not know, he was saved much unhappiness. He was also saved paltry misgiving in his days. If he could not help it, it was no fault for him. And as he did not know anything about it, he did not experience it, and was not unhappy about it, and his mind was not unclean with new names for ancient qualities of man. He fared forward with a bright mind."

"Stay, stay," cried Mac Taill in a sudden agony that silenced all. "Finn was not always good. Finn was not always just and noble and pure. He fell by the way and stumbled into evil. Unhappy men that we are, we are all the same in this, and mar our most beautiful desires with acts that shame us and drive us to despair." He beat his breast as he spoke with one hand, and plucked his beard with the other. "I am worse in this than any other. Did not his conscience convict him? It is both the judge in eternity and the purge in time of all men. It is the witness in man of God. Did it not throw him into the abyss of remorse?"

"Finn did not debase himself with recollection of the times when he was unworthy of himself. It was only his enemies who remembered these times, and by that we knew them for his enemies, and slew them instantly when we could. He left these times and forgot them, and mused on nobleness and the beauty of man. What use to recall them when done? That is only to continue them. Remorse is a waste of time and power better given to the making of what is memorable."

Oisin spoke with a pride that Iserninus instantly perceived to be pagan, and with a few sharp words he dispelled the fatal illusion.

"God does not forget," he said. "He never forgets," he repeated. "The wages of sin are death, and the best commentators are decided that this death is banishment from his presence in the flames of fire."

"There is no accounting for the gods," Oisin remarked with resignation. "Nor is there any avoiding them. They are the enemies of men, and that is why they remember."

"That is not so," Padraic mac Alphurn said gently. He also spoke with firmness and surety, for he had been preparing his mind. "It is so with pagan gods, who are the imaginings of demons. It is not so with the One Only and True God, Who is One in Three. He is not man's enemy, but man's lover. He forgets. Finn mac Cumhal could not always forget, O Oisin?"

"That is so," Oisin said. "We are nothing but our memories, and our memories are we. We cannot go outside our destinies, and we cannot go outside our memories, for our memories are our destinies. It is sometimes a pity, but it cannot be helped."

"That," answered Padraic in the same spirit of confidence, "is the happy news I have to tell you. For God, the True God, One in Three, can forget. He can go outside the law of memory, and He can bring us also outside that law. He will wash out the memory of all that is evil, leaving only what is beautiful and worthy of memory. That is His salvation."

"That," said Oisin doubtfully, "would be a good thing to do, no question about it."

"It is a great mystery," said Padraic.

"It must be," said Oisin.

"I will explain it to you," said Padraic, "and you will believe, and you will be baptised, and you will be saved. I see it all perfectly plain before me."

"I would not like to part with all my memories," said Oisin, looking doubtfully at Padraic in fear of his druidic experiment.

"Only those memories that are sinful," Padraic assured him.

"But some of my sinful memories are also pleasant," Oisin said, and his tone was stubborn.

"Only those that are evil then," Padraic eagerly replied, reluctant to stumble over a word apt for pagan misunderstanding.

"It is full of risk," Oisin still hesitated. "I do not like to part with any part of myself, and I am myself in virtue of my memories. I prefer to be myself than somebody else. I do not want to be a dog, and I do not want to be an angel. Oisin I am, and Oisin the son of Finn I would remain, whatever happens."

"Never fear," Padraic mac Alphurn said in glad confidence. "You will be born again in the spirit, and appear a perfect and eternal and beautiful Oisin. You will be a hero in the spirit. The joy of Tir-na-nOg is nothing to the joy that awaits you."

"I do not desire to be born again. I do not understand what this is, but I am sure it would be a most untimely act for me. Was Finn mac Cumhal born again?"

"Without doubt," said Padraic enthusiastically, and did not note the alarmed and angry glances Iserninus and Auxilius exchanged. "He died in a state of innocence."

"I, too, will die in a state of innocence, and whatever will come I will endure."

"You cannot," Padraic said. "It is too late. But nevertheless you will rise into a life when all evil will be cleansed from you—that is, from your memory. God is over all, and it is His love that can do this. It is hate that remembers; it is love that forgets."

He stopped. Then a thought whispered to him, and he accepted that thought as the movement of the spirit. His mind was filled with ardent light, and he misdoubted nothing. He leaned forward and said:

"Tell me, O hero, in what was Finn mac Cumhal greatest?"

"In what was he greatest? He was greatest in that he was Finn mac Cumhal."

"You mistake me," said Padraic mac Alphurn, not to be disappointed. "He lives his life in your memory. Tell

me, how do you wish chiefly to remember him? It is a
fine test."

IX

THE HOSPITALITY OF FINN

OISIN WAS SILENT. He was bent forward in deep
thought. His brow was wrinkled. Then he lifted his head,
the wrinkles departed, and his eyes were open and clear
like a hawk's while he looked into Padraic mac Alphurn's
own.

"I will not tell a lie," he said. "Finn mac Cumhal was
greatest when he gathered all men about him in his house
and gave them all he had."

Padraic's heart was uplifted with joy when he heard
these words, for he had foreknowledge that this was what
Oisin would say. It was because he felt the foreknowledgable spirit come into his mind that he had asked his
question. He waited to hear its whisper before he spoke
again. Then he said:

"He had a mansion of wonder, no doubt."

"O bishop," Oisin answered, "you may well say so.
The house of the Ard-Ri of the Five-fifths of Ireland was
not fashioned more delicately or built so large. It was set
in spacious Almhuin, in Laighen of the valleys and the
plains. Little avail for me to describe it. A poet would not
exhaust its beauties in a year of poems. Yet, the excellence
is not in a building but in its entertainment; and that

house had four doors. Four great roads came to the four
doors, one from the east and one from the west, one from
the south and one from the north. All men who came by
those roads came to those doors, and all men who came
to those doors came into the house. There was food for
each man, and there was entertainment for each man,
and there was a bed for each man. They came when they
came and they went when they would. There was nobody
to constrain them, for Finn sat in the midst of all. It
was a beacon and a welcome, the same house. It was an
encouragement and an upholding. Travellers on the road
at night would see that house from a great distance; they
would see into its doors that always were open; they
would see the mighty fire that burned in it and the torches
that stood in the walls, and the light fluttering on the
shields and weapons where they hung; and they would
see Finn among his guests entertaining them; and they
would give a shout for Finn and hasten on the road. If
it was an enemy, Finn would entertain him; and if it was
a friend, Finn could not give him more. For Finn never
turned any man away. In that Finn was greatest of all;
for every man came as he was, long men and short men,
lean men and round men, happy men and cross men, wise
men and men not so wise, men to make poems and men
to make laws and men to make nothing at all, men to
teach and men to listen, upstanding men and downfalling
men, blue-eyed men and brown-eyed men and grey-eyed
men and green-eyed men and straight-eyed men and

crooked-eyed men, and every sort and condition and manner of men. Finn did not accuse them because they were not as he was. He did not accuse them for their fate or their destiny. Finn received them all. Whatever the difference among themselves, they were the same in his welcome. In that Finn was greatest of all."

"And sick men?" asked Padraic mac Alphurn.

"Sick men and sound men," said Oisin.

"And sorrowful men?"

"Sorrowful men and gladsome men."

"Did he heal the sick and cure the sorrowful?"

"His welcome healed and cured. There is virtue to heal and cure in a welcome that is not measured."

"The halt and the blind and the weak of wit?"

"They, too. The doors were open to the white roads in the beautiful plain."

"Did Finn cure the halt and the blind and the weak of wit?"

X

THE HOSPITALITY OF EARTH AND HEAVEN

WHEN PADRAIC ASKED THIS QUESTION, Oisin lifted his body and looked sternly at him with his two eyes grey-bright with anger. But he said nothing. His silence was louder than his previous speech had been. It flowed from him in swift waves that beat upon the shores

of every man's mind that was present, and made him restless because of a storm from a distance.

Yet Padraic mac Alphurn was immune because he was
bewitched by his foreknowledgable spirit. He checked the
confident smile that came wreathing his lips, and said
with pride and dignity:

"I ask you this, O hero, because my Master also received all men that came to Him."

"Is that so?" Oisin said coldly. "And was His entertainment as wide as His welcome, for it is easy to welcome
without substance?"

"It was," said Padraic mac Alphurn; "and it was wider.
On one occasion he entertained thousands of men, women
and children that came to him. They all ate and were filled,
and none went empty away. It was with two little loaves
and three small fishes He did it."

Oisin looked again at Padraic in cold anger, but when
he saw the ardent light that lit Padraic's countenance his
expression changed.

"It was, no doubt, a good way," he said, "if one could
do it; but it was not very costly."

"It was," said Padraic, "the costliest test of all. It cost
love. Those that came halt went leaping away. Those that
came blind went on the road constructing intricate poems
on clouds and flowers and every sort of wonderful thing.
Those that came dumb went wild with language, and had
to be knocked on the head in the end to be silenced at all.
Those that came weak in the wit started to talk so sen-

sibly that folk soon grew weary of listening to them, and they were left refreshing one another with their wisdom. Every man went away satisfied; and satisfaction, O hero, is the rarest thing in the world, for it has to be proof against paucity and excess; having a great inclination to lose the delicate balance that is required. Therefore, was not my Master greater than Finn mac Cumhal?"

It was easily known that Padraic mac Alphurn was confident because of his gaiety. This was not only to be heard in his happy speech, but was also to be seen in his happy pride of manner. The gaiety had a conquering quality, and Oisin was almost subdued into receiving his doctrine. But an ardent loyalty burned in his heroic bosom. It saved him. It bubbled up in his aged heart like a well-spring of youth, and broke out into the following reply:

"It is a pity your Master to be dead, for there are wits yet that are weak, shanks yet that are crooked and eyes yet that are sore. Finn mac Cumhal was but a man, and did what a man could. He gave freely and asked no return. It was not only to the fellowship of the Fianna that he gave."

"Ah," cried Padraic, "be not for ever talking of the Fianna. They have passed you like a mist, and the sun is shining over your head. It was my Master made the sun and the moon, each in its own place. Was it only for a few He made them, and is not that hospitality large enough? It was He formed the heavens, He that created the universe, and He, O hero, that gave might to the warrior. It was He that strewed blossoms over the trees, that lifted the elm to be lofty, that squared the oak to be strong, that decorated the holly to be beautiful. It was He that modelled the flowers and filled their cups with overflowing fragrance. It was He that brought fish into the lakes, and sent the deer leaping through the woods with delicate bounds. It was He that formed field and grass—the spiky grasses that lift their heads against the sky like an army when you lie in the field under the sun. It was He made the little birds, and it is in His praise they fill the valleys with invisible song; the thrush of Gleann-an-Sgail and the blackbird of Leitreac Laoi and the wren that will not bend the littlest twig. Does He not, too, give freely, and is His entertainment for a few or for all?"

"Was it He then that made the world?" Oisin asked in the utmost surprise.

"He and no other," Padraic answered; "for He is God over all. The earth is His and the fullness thereof, and without Him was nothing made that was made."

"Did He make Finn mac Cumhal?"

"He did indeed."

"That was a good thing to do, for Finn was the most generous man that ever lived. Recreation of spirit and mind he never begrudged to any man."

"O hero," exclaimed Padraic mac Alphurn in the inconceivable ardour that urged him towards Oisin, "shall not the Giver prove greater than His own gifts? The greatest goodness that was in Finn was but a ray from the beam of light Himself is. If He were not, there could be no goodness in Finn, for He is the goodness that is in every man. Could there be weapons without a smithy? Can there be light without a sun? He is the original of all goodness, and therefore He is God. He is the fountain of all beauty and healing. The hospitality that was in Finn is nothing to the hospitality that is in God, by the same token that the sword is not more than the smithy and light is less than the sun."

"All roads led to the hospitality of Finn," said Oisin a little sullenly, for he did not wish it to be known that he did not understand Padraic's words as well he seemed to do.

"Do not all roads lead to death, and what is death but the portal of the house of God?" Padraic answered triumphantly.

XI

TRIUMPH AND ACCLAMATION

WHEN OISIN HEARD THESE WORDS, the effect on him was most remarkable. At first he did not mind them, for the deepest wisdom flows inland to the mind through a thousand inlets of the brain like a tide pressed on from utmost distances. Then he sprang aloft, standing beside

the astonished Padraic like an elm beside a holly bush.
Padraic looked up to see what was the matter. The two
had been sitting beside one another on a long, low, oaken
bench; and so, in order to look up, he had to lean his head
back at a most unepiscopal angle.

He was just in time to see Oisin's beard fall back on his
breast like a drift of discoloured snow, and to see his
excited eyes and high cheek-bones appear greyly and
pinkly over the drift as Oisin bent to roar down at him:

"I see it now. The portals of earth are the gates of
heaven. To be sure, nothing could be clearer. The portals
of earth are the gates of heaven." Several times he roared
this down at Padraic, who leant back on his arms looking
up at him. For he had perceived that Padraic mac Alphurn
had confirmed something himself had said, and no greater
proof of another's rightness has yet been discovered. He
was delighted to find Padraic fill his expectations of a just
man and a true. "So simple and so true," he roared. "The
portals of earth are the gates of heaven. I am beholden
to you for your sweet revelation, O bishop—do you hear
me?" Padraic, of course, could not help hearing, since it
is recorded in the books that he was heard five miles distant
by an old couple walking the road, who fell out as to
whether it was or was not thunder, and whose falling out
is proof of their hearing. Yet, it was only by way of
punctuation that he said this. So, "Do you hear me?" he
roared. "I am beholden to you for your revelation. I see it

now. That is where Finn mac Cumhal is now. And Oscar, the brave Oscar, my son Oscar, Oscar the matchless. And Caoilte, the gentle Caoilte, Caoilte of the eyes like a caress. And all the Fianna, the mighty, death-dealing Fianna of Ireland. Feasting and making merry."

"I do not know about feasting," Padraic mac Alphurn said, wishing that Oisin would sit down, for he found it extremely awkward leaning back looking upwards at a man whose grey eyes and pink cheeks looked at him from somewhere near the roof, over the drift of a yellow-white beard. Still, he smiled proudly and said: "I do not know about feasting. Nothing is revealed about that. But that is where they are, for the hospitality of my Lord is more than the hospitality of a thousand Finns, and therefore Finn must house with Him at last. Do you not see?"

"I do see," Oisin cried. "I see it, I see it now. It is what I would wish to believe, and therefore it must be true."

"That is so," Padraic said, as happy as he. "For my God also created the heart of man, and He would not plant desires He could not hope to fulfil."

"To be sure," Oisin cried again. "The portals of earth are the gates of heaven. And Finn mac Cumhal was noble and generous."

"And my God must resume His own goodness and cleanse all evil at last," continued Padraic, trembling with excitement.

"I must make haste to die," exclaimed Oisin then in

an outburst of haste, as if he were prepared to die then and there without further notice. "I am tired of earth when I think of what heaven is. Besides which I am old, and therefore have few senses left for pleasure, whether of earth or of Tir-na-nOg. Heaven is the place for me. I must die, for I long to be with Finn and Oscar and Caoilte and all the brave Fianna."

"It is God Whom you must wish to see," Padraic chided him, though not in anger, for it is difficult to be angry leaning back on one's arms looking upwards, and it is harder to be angry with eyes so bright and cheeks so eager.

"I do not know much about Him, never having seen Him, and it is that which men have seen they desire to renew. O bishop whom I love, when I have seen Him I will desire Him; but now I desire to see Finn. Could I not die at once? I would be easy to slay, so old as I am. Is there no one to contest with me?"

"You cannot die now," Padraic exclaimed in alarm. "You are not yet baptised."

"Finn was not baptised."

"Finn died in innocence, but of good heart."

"I will die in innocence."

"You cannot. I have told you it is too late, for the truth has been revealed to you, and now the good heart will not avail you any longer, for the believing mind is more than the good heart. You must believe and be baptised."

"I will believe and be baptised. I will do these things

at once, in case I should miss Finn mac Cumhal," he exclaimed in the sincerest alarm. "Why did I leave it for so long?"

"You must receive true doctrine."

"I will receive it."

"You must be taught."

"I will do that too."

"And be rightly instructed, for without right instruction there is no salvation."

"That too. Anything that is necessary. I am in terror to miss Finn mac Cumhal and Caoilte mac Ronan and Oscar my own son. Instruct me now. Does it take long? I will repeat anything you say, and do whatever you decide."

He stood high above Padraic with his arms outstretched, supplicating him. His tongue supplicated, his eyes supplicated, his arms supplicated, and everything about him supplicated. Such a picture of true repentance` Padraic mac Alphurn had never seen in all his lengthy experience. Therefore he sprang upon his two feet without an instant's delay, and seized Oisin by the hand.

"I will begin now, without further delay," he said. "It never does to miss the precious mood of repentance, lest it should not happen again."

And forthwith he led Oisin into a private room apart. For Padraic mac Alphurn was a man of great decision of character, who never, as the saying is, let the grass grow under his feet.

XII

HOW THE OTHERS RECEIVED THE TRIUMPH

THIS UNIQUE SCENE, without a rival, as it has been admitted to be, in the annals of salvation, left the others stricken with astonishment. After Padraic mac Alphurn had left the hall, leading Oisin by the hand, there was a lengthy period of silence, during which no man looked at his fellow.

The silence flowed on lengthier and lengthier, and still no man looked at his fellow. The silence was like the silence of space, because it was empty even of unspoken thoughts. These had been expelled by the utterness of astonishment. After a scene so unique it was only fitting that the silence should also be unique.

Then Iserninus leaned over and whispered in Auxilius' ear. When that thin sibilance reached Seachnall he drew near, and began also to whisper. Then Soichell joined the company. But he did not whisper. He ony listened, as if it did not matter to him what was said, but that it was no harm to hear it.

Hearing the whispering Mac Taill lifted his head and looked across at the party, but he found the sight apparently so unpleasant that he rose and left the room, making for the open air.

When he had got outside he heard a sound, and found

Brogan beside him. For Brogan had also found the sight unpleasant, and had also left the room.

"I like that ancient hero," said Mac Taill, looking down at Brogan beside him. "I must say I like the ancient hero very well. There is something about him particularly frank and natural. I like him."

"I like him, too," said Brogan. "I always did, since the first morning when he began to fling chairs. His stories will make a great book for me to leave to posterity. His replies, too, make very good dialogue. They look very well in manuscript. But I misdoubt that the company inside is hatching some mischief, all the same."

"Do you tell me so?" said Mac Taill, looking at him out of his beard in extreme surprise.

THE FIFTH BOOK

I

A POINT IN THEOLOGY

"I will call upon my dear Brother Iserninus to speak," Padraic mac Alphurn said, directing at Iserninus so concentrated a glance that it was even a test of holiness to have withstood it at all.

To the ignorant it would have appeared from Padraic mac Alphurn's manner that he was angry. Indeed, in a manner of speaking, he was angry; but it was not the anger of the flesh, which is full of sin, but the anger of an upright man, which is proof that there resides in him a well-spring of righteousness.

This much of cause he had for anger, that his plans were thrown into disarray. And this much added inducement there was, that he was now two nights and days without sleep. If, therefore, his anger had been of the flesh, it might have been winked at by his Almighty Master, Who in His wisdom designed the mortal frame of a certain limited endurance beyond which, as His Omniscience knows, it is not responsible for a breakdown of the machinery so exquisitely built. But it was not only anger of the flesh. It was the anger of uprightness, and he had very good reason for it, as his conscience infallibly averred.

He had spent the whole night instructing Oisin. He had sat on Oisin's bed repeating phrases, and Oisin had sat beside him repeating after him with equal earnestness. He had sat almost in Oisin's lap, looking up at him with eager solicitude, and Oisin had sat bent over him, staring down at him in pained attention. The long night they had sat thus, first one speaking a phrase, and then the other earnestly saying it back again.

For the lesson had by necessity to be oral. As a boy, Oisin, over two hundred years before, had been destined for none of the professions—neither to be a Brehon nor a Seanchaidhe—but for the army; and so he had not wasted time to learn Script, but had been instructed only in ungrammatical Ogham, suitable for epitaphs and despatches and other such brevities for which care of diction is not required. So he was now at a loss. For no Christian treatises, needing extraordinary care in nice points of logic, doctrinal, canonical and liturgical, had been written, or for that matter could have been written, in Ogham. Hence these two eager hearts had been compelled to beat together, and these ardent lips constrained to repeat phrases together in voice and antiphone in the bitter cold, unheeding the darkness that pulsed away, as darkness will pulse away whether it is minded or not.

Even now the lesson was being continued. In the

woods beside the house, Brogan and Oisin were walking
up and down, Brogan repeating phrases out of a book and
Oisin repeating them back again.By this time, Oisin was
thoroughly dazed and did not know what he was saying or
what was being said to him. But he had a traditional
memory, as became one of the old school, and the strength
and exactness of the traditional memory are well known.
He could by now repeat whole chapters of what he had
learnt. He knew all the cues. He had not the least notion
what it all meant. He had even passed the stage when
some of the questions in his catechism had occurred to
him as singularly futile, and some of the answers as of
a baffling simplicity. But what he had learnt, he had
learnt. He made no mistake. He never mixed the answers with the questions to which they were the answer.
He had mastered question and answer in blocks together,
so that each question evoked its own answer without the
least chance of an error however trickily the questioner
might have dodged to and fro among the possibilities.
For this, undoubtedly, he had to thank his traditional
memory. For though his mind was utterly dazed, till he
did not know whether he was sleeping or walking, and
though his pagan comprehension had not the least understanding of the awful mysteries that were being expounded
to him, yet he continued walking up and down with Brogan, who hurried beside him, saying phrases after him, and
repeating question and answer in blocks together so as to
know the cues, until he was fast on the way to becoming

the most word-perfect student in theology among them all.

The day was very cold, but he did not mind this. The woods were decked with beauty, for the brush of Autumn had painted them in yellow, orange, saffron, blood-red and all the hues of tender reminiscence. But did he give any heed to them? Not a bit. The last lonely thrush was musing in the tree-tops, as it is well known that last lonely thrushes have always mused in the tree-tops of every sad and beautiful scene. But as far as Oisin was concerned, it mused in vain. Oisin wanted only to renew his sight of his father, Finn mac Cumhal, of his son Oscar, of the gentle Caoilte, and to taste the joys of heaven. By comparison with these things, earth was as nothing. So he paced beside Brogan, and Brogan hasted beside him, repeating phrases out of an illuminated, though not in his dazedness very illuminating, book. Brogan thought he had never met so tireless a man. He knew of a certainty that he had never met any man of so powerful and punctual and precise a memory.

In view of this docile and anxious disciple he had plucked as a brand from the burning, and of the example even now being given both of his anxiety and of his docility, not to mention his abstraction from the things of this world into the things of the next, it is not surprising that Padraic should have been angered, or that his anger should have been of the righteous variety. For Iserninus had raised some nice points as to the debate of yesterday. He had spoken, not indelicately, of saving a soul under false pretences, and had questioned whether souls could be saved by that method at all. Not content with this, he had insinuated, in that dry way of his, that an act almost amounting to a sin had been committed in setting the salvation of Oisin's soul above the truth of doctrine. Better let the whole world perish than that the truth be impugned. Let the truth be preached whatever happened. Only thus, and not by pandering to human affection, or by truckling to human philosophy, could it be clearly known what souls were destined for eternal salvation. Therefore, Oisin should be recalled and informed that Finn mac Cumhal was not in heaven; that it was a misapprehension to say he was; but that he was in hell, where he was even now enduring the tortures of the eternally damned.

To this Auxilius had added his word. Broadly he agreed with his brother Iserninus. But he looked at the question from another point of view. The Church desired all men to be saved, because the more who were saved the more powerful its membership. Therefore it was right to welcome Oisin if one could. But this did not affect Finn mac Cumhal and his wild comrades, who were dead, and whose souls only were now in question. What had they to do with the Church? And this raised another question of gravest importance. For the Church was the Bride of Christ. Was it possible to think of Finn mac Cumhal as part of the Bride? The thing was unthinkable, besides being, as his brother Iserninus had said, contrary to doctrine. Therefore, on grounds of formal correctness involving future organisation, he agreed with his brother Iserninus that Oisin should be clearly told that Finn was not part of the Bride, but that he was as his brother Iserninus had said, and as he had to admit with deepest sorrow was the case.

Seachnall stated how he stood in the matter. He said he agreed with his brother Iserninus for the reasons his brother Iserninus had given. He also agreed with his brother Auxilius, and thought his brother Auxilius had made out a very strong case. It was true, to be sure, that there were other sides to the case. Anyway it would do no harm to recall Oisin in order that they might find out exactly how they stood.

To all this, Padraic mac Alphurn had answered brusquely, being tired, that he did not agree with any of them. All the signs pointed to the fact that Finn mac Cumhal was in heaven. He was a good man according to his lights, and had died in a state of innocence. As to doctrine, he was of opinion that sound doctrine was, after all, not a matter of learning, of which it was true he had little, but a matter of sound sense, of which he hoped he had more than some others whom he could name.

This he had said, being tired, and brushed the argument imperiously aside. He was that sort of a man. But Iserninus stopped him, and said in his cold, insistent way that this raised a matter of deepest gravity. Sound doctrine was not a matter of sound sense, but of heavenly sense, which to human ears might sound nonsense. This was a matter to be argued in counsel together. They were all equally bishops, he reminded his brother Padraic, whom in the Lord he loved, and whom in the Church he revered, but to whom he would gently say that these were matters to be argued in counsel together as a bench of bishops, not to be dismissed by one of them offhand in this manner. Oisin's soul was important unquestionably. But the truth was more important. He appealed to the discipline of the Church, which was not the discipline of one man but the discipline of Truth discovered in counsel together. Then, having consulted together, they could see Oisin further, and not rashly baptise him under distinctly false pretences.

Therefore, Padraic mac Alphurn had called the bishops together. None but bishops were present—himself presiding—Iserninus, Auxilius, Seachnall and Mac Taill sitting round in an equal and impartial circle. Therefore he now directed a concentrated glance towards Iserninus and said to him:

"I will call upon my dear brother Iserninus to speak."

II

THE POINT IN THEOLOGY IS CONTINUED

FINDING HIMSELF ADDRESSED IN THESE WORDS, Iserninus cleared his throat in a deprecating manner, and without any further delay, expressed himself in these words:

"Dear brother, as the matter now stands, this man Oisin

must not be baptised. The potency of baptism is such that once he has received the sacrament, nothing can keep him out of heaven. I have heard of these Fianna. I perceive that this man justifies all the reports I have heard. Consider this thing well, I urge of you. Once this man finds himself in heaven, unable to get out of it, with his father and son and past comrades in hell, I foresee that there will be the gravest possible disorder——"

"He may even consider himself cheated," interrupted Seachnall.

"He may," continued Iserninus. "I foresee from the kind of man he is—and have not his own words only too plainly revealed his character to us?—that he will not desire to remain there. It is not possible to resist the law of election and predestination. Only those who in the Eternal Wisdom were chosen for that blessed state will be fitted to endure it. Others will find it too much for them. They will not be able to rise to the joy required of them. Beware, then, how we import under false pretences this ancient roysterer into that august company. When he finds that his boon companions are not there, he will want to get out, and the whole peace of heaven will be upset because of him."

Seachnall lifted his hand. His honoured age and hymnful capacity gave his words a peculiar authority among them.

"That is most true," he said. "It is a grave responsibility. This man has given no proof of being quit of carnal desires, but has even, in our hearing, openly exulted in them. He has wished for heaven for the final consummation of those desires instead of for the lasting refutation of them. Have we not heard him? Is it likely, then, that he will be content with heaven when he gets there? Will he not rather bitterly upbraid us, and will we not be put to shame before the heavenly host, both for a grave error of judgment and for upsetting the eternal harmony? It would prove a most distressing experience for us. The responsibility is very great."

Auxilius had been waiting for Seachnall to finish. He, therefore, vigorously applauded his concluding words to ensure that he would not continue, and at once addressed the attentive company.

"All this," he said, "is based on an important truth. It is concerned with the validity of baptism, the responsibility of which, as my dear brother Seachnall has pointed out with such truth, is reposed in our hands. Ours is the Apostolic Succession. Whom we bind is bound. Whom we loose is loosed. How wise, then, were the words of our Blessed Master that on this rock would be built His Church, for without an absolute authority of this kind, lasting in its extent, and beyond the power of any to evade, it would be quite impossible to think of erecting any organisation so complicated as the Church. Not all His words are capable of so universal an application. Some of them are not so extensive, and must be understood in their context clearly. Others of them are not to be enforced without wisdom. Others again are true only in spirit, and would lead to civil disorder if preached by unauthorised persons. Who is to judge if not the Church? How is the Church to exist or continue without authority to bind or loose for ever? We see, then, how wise was our Master when He made this the rock on which to build His Church. All whom we send to heaven must remain there. All whom we send to hell cannot escape. And this, my brethren, is done by the sacrament of baptism, which is the act by which we accomplish the mystery, for if it once got abroad that that act was not sufficient, there would be an end of all authority."

"It is not the form of the sacrament that binds, but the spirit of it," Mac Taill's deep voice interrupted him at this point.

Auxilius paused for a moment before dealing with this interruption. There was an uneasy silence.

"That," he said, "I regard as a cardinal heresy. For what is heresy but the unloosening of authority? Heresy is not the teaching of wrong doctrine, for what is heresy at one time may not be heresy at another. Heresy is the teaching of the wrong doctrine at the wrong time, when that doctrine is not permitted to be taught; and so it is not heresy in respect of doctrine, but heresy in respect of authority, being a disregard of the authority at that time available. Anything that weakens the power of the Church is a heresy; and so I have no hesitation in describing as a heresy any teaching that exalts the spirit above the form. For where would the power of the Church be but for her authority? And where would the authority of the Church be but for the lasting and only efficacy of the form?

Men would escape into private judgments, and anarchy would prevail."

"We shall be here all day if we go into these subjects," said Padraic mac Alphurn irritably. "What has all this got to do with the hero Oisin?"

"I accept the correction," said Auxilius with great dignity, "in the spirit of tenderness in which it is meant. I am asked what has this got to do with Oisin? In my answer, therefore, I accept as true beyond refutation that the form binds for ever if administered by the right persons—or even, as some authorities aver, if administered by the wrong persons—as long as the form is that which has been ordained by authority of the Church. Consider then what we are about to do with this preposterous old man, who has wandered out of his age into ours. Is it not only too clear that he is an anachronism? His motives are not as ours, nor are his desires the same. He does not desire to dwell among the blessed in heaven, but only to see Finn mac Cumhal. He does not hope to gaze upon the face of God, but merely to converse with his son, who died a touching but disorderly death. I would not like to answer for what he might do when he discovered that all his old companions were in eternal torment. He has a most erroneous conception of fidelity. And the Almighty would be restricted from destroying him by our act. I say it is a heavy responsibility. It threatens the very security of heaven."

how can heaven be so vulnerable

Mac Taill rose to speak. He spoke with unexpected vigour and with expected incoherence.

"It seems to me," he said, "that heaven will be comprised of all sorts. I plead for a place for Oisin, because I am sure many will appreciate his presence there, if only because he is copious of good stories. I do not blame you for it, my dear brethren, because you are not familiar with our history, but toleration was always held in traditional respect among our people. Our very battles, which so sadly mar our record, were based on mutual courtesy and forbearance. Heaven is the place where all good things are preserved, and there are many qualities in Oisin, a little out of date perhaps, that one would wish to see preserved. There are many people on whom, by the blessed sacrament of baptism, we have conferred immortality and glory in whom one's interest cannot be very great, for, though they have many respectable qualities, they have commonplace souls. God knows I do not blame them—who am I to distribute blame among men?—but such is the fact. Perhaps I have a commonplace soul myself. But since the responsibility has, in the Eternal Wisdom, been entrusted to us, let us take our courage in our hands and introduce into heaven at least one such man as this admirable hero Oisin. I do believe he would be of general interest."

He ceased as abruptly as he began. But as nobody knew what he was talking about, and as it is doubtful if himself knew, nobody paid any attention to what he said.

III

A MATTER OF WORDS

THERE WAS SILENCE IN THE ASSEMBLY. Padraic mac Alphurn was expected to speak, but seemed disinclined to do so. One after another they all looked at him with furtive care, but it was impossible to know of what he was thinking.

Then Iserninus ventured to remind him of the point of the argument. His voice fell into the silence chilly, like an icicle in a cave. He said:

"He will not be content to remain in heaven. He will surely want to get out. I know the man. But it is written that there will be a great gulf fixed——"

"Why will he want to get out?" Padraic mac Alphurn asked suddenly and sharply. "Answer me that."

"Because," said Seachnall, stepping in and speaking in a mild and careful manner, "of the kind of man he is, and of his evident distaste for the mild joys of the blessed, in the first place; and in the second place, because he will not find Finn and his company there, as he has been falsely led to hope. "

"I do not see," said Mac Taill, lifting his head again and speaking as out of a dream, "why Finn mac Cumhal should not be there. Why should that be assumed? Companies may only be potent when they express a coherent and uniform idea, but they are only interesting when they are comprised of interesting people. In heaven, my dear brethren, there will be no more need for potency, for sin will have been overcome. There will thus be an opportunity for interesting people. It seems to me, from all we have heard of Finn mac Cumhal, that heaven will not be able to do without a personality of such distinction and rarity. No place where we creatures will have to abide eternally can afford to exile from its precincts the really interesting people. Let us recall that by its nature distinction is abnormal, and the abnormal is the interesting, and interest creates happiness. I confess that I myself desire to meet Finn mac Cumhal, and several others of the Fianna, in heaven. Am I then wrong in this? Is that desire, which I believe to be pure, a sin?"

"Our dear brother Mac Taill," said Padraic mac Alphurn, "has expressed himself with Celtic fire and earnestness. I understand him to mean that he believes Finn mac Cumhal to be in heaven. That is the point. If Finn mac Cumhal is in heaven, then Oisin will not desire to get out. My dear brother Iserninus," he said sternly, "has suggested that I have saved, or am about to save, Oisin's soul under false pretences——"

"False pretences, not in intention, but in fact," Iserninus interrupted hastily.

"False pretences neither in intention nor in fact," Padraic mac Alphurn said. "Finn mac Cumhal is in heaven. He died in innocence and of a good heart in an era before these qualities could be defined by acceptance or rejection of the doctrine we are charged to preach. If Finn mac Cumhal is in heaven, then all is well in regard to Oisin, and we waste time in discussing the matter."

"The question cannot be dismissed so easily," said Auxilius. "The Church must decide whether Finn is in heaven."

"Is it not God Who will decide that?" asked Mac Taill in a tone of astonishment.

"In a manner of speaking that is so," said Auxilius; "but actually not. He has resigned that matter into the hands of the Church. Whom we bind is bound. Whom we loose is loosed. It might be said that this cannot come of effect prior to the beginning of the Apostolic Succession, or the speaking of those august words. But I can show that it does. For if we are to speak with authority as to the conditions under which this man Oisin is to be bound or loosed, then we must be in a position to make those conditions absolute. Once admit doubt into our decisions and authority is undone."

"Consider, my dear brother," said Iserninus, addressing Padraic with noteworthy energy, "the extreme danger of the doctrine you have just announced. If men could get to heaven by dying in innocence and of a good heart, then where is our vocation gone? The unique virtue of the doctrine has been impugned that we have been charged to deliver to mankind sunk in sin."

"That is so," said Seachnall. "Undoubtedly that is so. Our special character disappears, and salvation is reduced to mere goodness, which, according to our preaching, is proof of the exceeding sinfulness of sin. Have we not always taught that the merely good man needs the virtue of ordinance and sacrament not less than the reprobate sinner? Is what we have taught true, or is it false?"

"It is true," said Padraic mac Alphurn in a great perplexity. "But it is true <u>since</u> the preaching of the Gospel."

Auxilius rose to his feet in great excitement. He said:

"Before or since, what does it matter? Reflect on the peril if such teaching as this once got abroad. Men would fly from us as from a plague. They would say we were bringing a responsibility to them they did not desire. They would say we darkened their lives, and that it was more blessed to live outside our influence than within it. Instead of emancipating them from sin we would be merely endowing them with its penalties. Our strongest argument would be turned against us. Salvation would become a menace. We have already seen the effect of such an idea on this preposterous old hero. He said he would die in innocence. Naturally. Everyone would determine to die in innocence, and then what hope would there be of organising the Church? My dear brethren, I urge you to consider this. We cannot be too firm. It is even essential for the future of the Church that Finn mac Cumhal be bound in hell."

This powerful reasoning, supported by so evident a sincerity, had a strong effect on Padraic mac Alphurn, as was plain to see from his manner of astonishment and distress.

"But consider, my dear brother," he urged, "the common-sense of the matter. Finn mac Cumhal was a good man. He lived according to the lights vouchsafed him. Besides which he is a national hero [Is he to be penalised for the age in which he was born? That would be clearly unjust, for he did not choose to be born then, but it was appointed that he should be born at a time when it may not have suited him. Some people had to be born then, or the Christian age in this country could never have come about in the flowing of time. In that sense he actually contributed to the bringing about of the Christian age. Is he to be consigned to hell by us for this?] I allow that some of his acts do not commend themselves to me; but a time in purgatorial pains would suffice for this. But the deep offence of rejecting our teaching cannot be charged against him, for there was no such teaching for him to reject. In short," he added, with regained confidence, "I appeal to the common-sense of the matter."

A grey light shone on Iserninus' face as he rose to reply.

"As the heaven is high above the earth, so is the Divine Wisdom above mortal wisdom. For this cause is it written that not many wise are called, nor many learned, but rather the humble and the lowly. It is not difficult to see the reason for this. It is not necessary for Divine Wisdom to confute this common-sense to which appeal has now been made, and I will not attempt to do so, for being equipped with omnipotence, it will dominate all things in the end, and will take pleasure in bringing the wise to nought and trampling the proud to dust. I am sure that my dear brother Seachnall will agree with me in this."

Appealed to in this way, Seachnall's features grew grave with responsibility, and he answered in these words:

"It is one thing to say that what we teach is such manifest common-sense that it should claim the adherence of all men, but it is quite another, it seems to me, to say that because a proposition appears to be manifest common-sense should therefore be incumbent on us to accept it, much less to preach it." He reflected a moment. "Quite another," he added emphatically and firmly.

"For myself," said Auxilius in a ringing voice, "I would even call such a notion a heresy. In the first place, it appeals to private judgment, and so displaces authority. In the second place, it is not exigent, and whatever is not exigent is heretical. We cannot, at this critical stage of history, allow of this mode of escape."

Against so powerful a weight of authority, Padraic mac Alphurn was in sore distress. In his distress he appealed to Mac Taill.

"What does my dear brother Mac Taill say?" he asked.

"I suggest," said Mac Taill boldly, "that we call Oisin himself."

This proposal caused the extremest surprise in the assembly. Each bishop turned towards the speaker in wonder and bewilderment.

"To what end," asked Auxilius sharply, "should we call this man?"

"To the end," Mac Taill answered simply, "that he should tell us a story. He is singularly copious of good stories."

A smile came over Padraic mac Alphurn's face as he looked on the astonishment of the company.

"I perceive," he said, "the truth of the saying that the voice of the simple-hearted shall overcome the judgment of the wise. We will invite the hero. Our dear brother will bring him among us, and he shall tell us a story of Finn mac Cumhal. By that story we will decide which of us is right. It will be for a guide to us."

IV

OISIN'S EXPECTATION

OISIN CAME TO THE ASSEMBLY expecting the mysterious ritual that would instantly convey him to Finn mac Cumhal and the bands of the Fianna of Ireland. His extreme age was transfigured with the youthfulness of hope and bright desire. His steps were buoyant and eager. The movements of his lean body were sinuous and graceful. He did not know if the angel who would transport him to heaven would be anything like Niamh who conveyed him to Tir-na-nOg, or if the steed to carry him would be more superb and lusty than the steed which she had ridden. The passages read him by Brogan from the Apocalypse had filled him with grave misgivings as to the sex of these angels, and the steeds struck him as more picturesque and monstrous than practicable. Still, these were details. Each country had its own eccentricities of manners, of men and of beasts. Finn mac Cumhal would be the same; Oscar's beauty would be unchanged; and Caoilte's love was unchangeable. Their ancient virtues would be as fresh to him as morning dew; and for them he would gladly endure the peculiarities of a country inhabited by strange beings like the Great Whore of Babylon and the Unicorn of the Seven Stars, and great crowds that marched to and fro singing Holy, Holy, Holy.

Custom would assuage these oddities and wizardries of life in the new country. No custom could dent the edge of loving comradeship. The main thing was to get where Finn mac Cumhal was as quickly as possible, and Oisin came prepared to receive the queer rite that had been promised him for his learning. He was confident in himself. There had been nothing so heroic in his long life as his application during the past twenty-four hours. It would baffle the most learned of these bishops, he felt assured, to outwit him in what he had committed, by whole chapters, to memory. No matter how ambiguous the questions, or how mysterious the replies he was expected to make, he had them fitted each to each in all their possible variations. Word-perfect he was, and ready, utterly ready.

Great, therefore, was his dismay when he learned that the rite was to be postponed. It mollified him little to learn that the bishops wished to hear another tale about

Finn mac Cumhal. His disappointment was too keen for him to take pleasure even in the fact that these bishops were thus far interested in his great captain. Yet, being a hero, he accepted with sternness all ills of life as they came.

He asked, therefore, with the calm born of grievous disappointment, what kind of tale they wished to hear, since there were as many kinds of tales about Finn as there were berries in Autumn, and all of them true. To this, Mac Taill answered as quickly as eagerly that it would be extremely pleasant to have a tale of witchery and magic, if there were such a tale in Oisin's recollection. Now, Mac Taill was a man who had always pleased Oisin well, and so this was the tale he told.

V

THE TALE OF THE MYSTERIOUS CUP

"It was," he said, beginning slowly in the effort to put his disappointment heroically behind him, "once when we were hunting on Sliabh Fuaidh in the north that the deer went onwards before the men. On he went without falter in step or bound until he came to craggy Carraigin, and when we got to that place we did not know what way he had gone. We all parted different ways, and Finn mac Cumhal had the melodious Daire for his companion. It was in a druidic magical mist they

were, for Daire played a pitiful music and Finn sounded
his horn, and whatever way we went to meet that music
it was always behind us and never could we come near
them.

"It was then a gentle maid with cheeks like the rose
came to Finn. Her name was Glannluadh, and she came
to assist the two heroes. But while they held gentle converse they heard drowsy faery music chanted melodiously
by their side. 'How is this, O Finn mac Cumhal,' said the
noble princess, 'I am entirely pining away?' 'So am I, too,
O gentle woman,' said Finn. 'Nor am I quite well myself,'
quoth Daire. And with that they all slept in death's heavy
repose.

"When they recovered from their faints they saw themselves beside a golden fortress of powerful sway. Around
them rocked a rough-waved, greenish, stormy sea, and
across from the fortress towards them swam a corpulent
hero and a gentle maid. That corpulent hero and that
gentle maid seized these three and bore them within the
golden fortress. 'Why do you treat me thus?' said Finn,
'for it is not becoming in a hero not to be magnanimous
and just.' 'Dost thou remember slim Meargach of the
spears?' said this warrior. 'I am now to right that deed
on Cnoc-an-Air. My own name is Draoigheantoir, and
this is my sister Ailne, the wife of the same Meargach.'

"Sad was their state, then, for they lay in a dungeon
without food and without drink. 'How came you to elope
with Finn mac Cumhal?' asked Ailne of the gentle Glann-

luadh, 'and his own mild wife alive. To your like ignoble was the deed.' Then it was that Glannluadh told the truth of her story, that she did not know east or west, and never saw him before that time. So Ailne released Glannluadh, and received her in her own house, and was sister to her, 'For,' said she, ' 'tis likely that to be the truth.' "

At this point of Oisin's story Seachnall broke in with a sharp speech. It is recorded that what he said was:

"I think it most unlikely, indeed. How do we know that something did not happen? The circumstances were most suspicious."

Oisin stopped and looked over Seachnall with a hostile glance. He spoke with pride.

"Men do not see other men but through their own eyes. One man's idea of another man's character is the best expression of his own."

And Padraic mac Alphurn was troubled to see the angry light in Seachnall's eyes, for he knew how critical Seachnall's vote was afterwards to be. He waved to Oisin to continue, but Oisin was silent awhile, thinking on the strangeness of some men's judgments. Then he returned to his tale.

"When Glannluadh was set free, there was hope for Finn mac Cumhal, for she was grieved at his bondage, having once shared it herself. She persuaded Ailne to bring food to him, and she persuaded her to bring drink to him. And Ailne brought food to the two heroes, and she brought drink to them, so that they lived. The two noble women brought food and drink to the two death-weary men.

"When Draoigheantoir heard of this he asked the occasion of it, and Ailne answered that it was because of the lovely music that was to be had by Daire. Then Draoigheantoir desired to hear the music, for all men have some music in their hearts, even if the music be strange or the heart be strange. Therefore he loosed Daire and Finn from their spells, and Daire made music for him, too.

"It was how we the Fianna heard that music, and knew that it was the music of Daire. In every place we had searched for our comrades, and in every place it had failed us to find them. Then we arrived at a certain place, and we did not know that it was at this place, behind the veils of magic and the folding of the doors of earth, that Finn and Daire were held. We did not know it, for they were beyond the illusion of our eyes, until we heard the music that we knew to be Daire's, for Draoigheantoir had loosed him from his spell. And we gave one mighty shout of joy and a loud cry of battle forthwith.

"Draoigheantoir heard that loud shout, and he quickly put his spells on the two heroes, and he also put spells on us, and instantly we were all in the golden fortress, lifting our common wail together. For it was the will of Draoigheantoir to put us all into death without delay. Tears of blood were on the face of Finn mac Cumhal for the end he had brought to his comrades.

"One hundred and three Draoigheantoir slew, until he

came to Conan the Bald. Now, the world is of all sorts, and Conan was of the world. It was not his fault that he was as he was, big of speech and little of heart, and big and likewise bald of head. When he saw the other coming towards him with a lance both sharp and severe, he leapt from his thongs and left part of his posterior on the seat after him. 'Never put me to death,' he said sorrowfully and gloomily, 'till thou first heal my wounds.' It was little for Draoigheantoir to grant him his request, and he took him with him to heal him.

"Now we knew from Glannluadh that Draoigheantoir had a Cup of powerful spells. A druid of the Magical Cup he was, for by that Cup he wrought all his magic. When, therefore, he was come to his place he called to Ailne, 'Give me the Cup of the Powerful Spells till I heal the posterior wounds of this big bald man now in gloom.' So Ailne brought the Cup, and Draoigheantoir placed it in the hands of Conan the Bald. As for Ailne, she examined the back parts of Conan, and applied to them a large skin full of feathers, which adhered to that place for ever. To his rump it adhered, and he was never without his bye-name from that time out. Bald he was in head, but he was not bald behind.

"Then Draoigheantoir hastened back to make an end of the heroes, and Ailne hastened with him. Altogether they forgot that they had left the Cup uplifted in the hands of Conan the Bald, to whose backside the feathers did adhere. And Conan hid the Religious Cup, the Cup of Power, in his clothes and hastened after him.

"When Draoigheantoir saw him approach he asked him why he came. 'To see the death and departure of the Fianna,' answered Conan the Bald. 'And where is the Cup I left with you?' asked Draoigheantoir. 'In yon room after me,' answered Conan the Bald. Draoigheantoir fled to examine his treasures; but while he was gone, Conan the Bald applied the virtue of the Cup to us all and we were all free."

"By the virtue of the Cup you were free!" exclaimed Padraic mac Alphurn joyfully.

"By the virtue of the Cup we were all free," said Oisin.

"Success and benediction, O hero," Padraic mac Alphurn cried out. "It is a good tale. It is also I perceive a prophetic tale. It is a tale given at this moment for a sign and a guidance to us. Finn was saved by the virtue of this Cup?"

"Finn was saved by virtue of this Cup surely," answered Oisin, a little wondering at the enthusiasm of this grave bishop.

"And the Fianna were saved by the virtue and potency of this Cup?"

"The Fianna also were undoubtedly saved by the virtue and potency of the Cup."

"It is a sign sent from heaven," Padraic exclaimed. "It cannot be interpreted in any other way. Let this tale be written by thee, O Brogan."

"It is written already," said Brogan.

"Let it be carefully recorded."

"It shall be carefully recorded."

VI

THE INTERPRETATION OF THE TALE

WHEN OISIN was gone out again, Padraic mac Alphurn turned in grave and confident triumph to his brethren. He looked at them each in turn; but they all pretended deep reflection, and did not meet his glance, for each man knew in his heart that it was one of those glances that cannot be met without either truculency or smiling abasement. And yet it was but a proud and happy glance.

Even Mac Taill did not meet that glance, though he was aware that it began with him, and that it returned to him with an affection all the purer for its travel.

"This tale," said Padraic then, "has undoubtedly been sent for a sign to us. The dreams, my brethren, by which holy men in all the ages have been infallibly guided, in their perplexities, by the Most High God, Whose children and servants we are, were never so clear as the guidance given by this story. Ofttimes, it must be confessed, ribald men have said that the interpretations given to those dreams were fanciful and fantastic. The dreams interpreted by the divine skill vouchsafed to the Patriarch

Joseph were of that kind. The dreams interpreted by the
Prophet Daniel were, it has been alleged, even more so.
It has even been said by worthless men that the man who
appeared in a dream to the holy Apostle Paul telling him
to 'Come to Macedonia,' was no other than the blessed
Saint himself, and that he mistook for the divine leading
his own earthly inclination. These ribald sneers, my
brethren, may be set aside. The more obscure a dream,
the greater the divine gift in finding a meaning for it, and
we must not wonder if the ungodly are astonished both
by the dream and the meaning given to it. Yet, because
of such ribaldries, I perceive that God has of late made
His signs more plain to be read, and has given over to the
ungodly the signs that are difficult and recondite.

"It is said of one of the heroes of this nation that it
foretold bad luck for him if he met three old women on
the road dressed in red. Not dressed in purple, you will
observe, nor dressed in blue. Why red? No one can tell.
Yet, this hero died when he did meet three such old
women. The sign was a true one, but it was quite arbi-
trary and without meaning. It was said of another that if
he approached a cooking hearth to eat of its viands it
would be the end of him. Was a sign ever so strange, since
it is by the cooking hearth we live, not die? Yet, this man
died, and he was no less a hero than Cuchulain himself.

"Compare with this the sign given to the Blessed
Apostle Peter himself, when, as he slept awhile, a great
sheet was let down from heaven wherein was all manner

of four-footed beast, while a voice came to him bidding him 'Arise and eat.' We know the visitors he had just received; we know the ancient prejudices of his Hebrew heart; and the sign is clear as the sun when it shines in heaven.

"By this we know that, whereas the world has slipped back from simplicity to complexity, He Himself has advanced from complexity to simplicity. His signs are now simple; His hints have become obvious; there is always some outstanding symbol that cannot be mistaken. These things are, as I may say, the heavenly metaphors of the divine poem of mortal guidance. There was no mistaking the beasts whom the Creator in His wisdom made, but which the Hebrew prejudice misliked, for in the Hebrew tradition the unclean beast had been the symbol of the Gentile. This was a connecting link that could not be mistaken. There was certainly no mistaking the meaning when the ardent Saul of Tarsus was overthrown from his horse when setting out to persecute the children of God.

"And I, even I, have found it so; for there was no mistaking the children of this land who called to me for their salvation—not one man, be it remarked, who might be accused as my secret wish escaping in a dream, but a number of children, speaking not in the Roman tongue, but in the purest Gaelic, with which I was not very familiar. The sign was most clear then. And so it is now. Indeed, I may say I have never met a sign so remarkable. The symbol, the connecting link, could not be more direct and pertinent, my brethren. We did not ask this loveable old hero to tell this story. He chose it; and he chose when we were in a difficulty. I say he chose it because he was given it as a sign to us. He could not avoid this story. Let us consider, my brethren, what our difficulty was. We were exercised to know whether Finn mac Cumhal was or was not in heaven, whether he was or was not saved, whether the atonement made for all mankind did or did not avail for him. In a word, we were exercised to know if the shedding of blood was efficacious in his behalf. And what was the sign that was given to us? We were told a story of how, when he was captive and sore to death, he was liberated by the virtue and sacred potency of a mysterious Cup. Could there have been a connecting link more clear? For I need not remind you, my brethren, what the uplifting of the Cup signifies for us. Consider the story again. By whom was Finn mac Cumhal bound on this occasion so perilous for him? I noted that especially. He was held by an infernal being named Draoigheantoir, and Draoigheantoir, we know, means a wicked Spell-Binder. This Draoigheantoir tried to turn this Cup to his own evil and corrupt purposes, but the virtue of the cup overcame him, and the captive was liberated, as it was prophesied would be the case. There is no need for me to say more, my brethren, for the sign is clear, and only the dark of sight could fail to see it."

When Padraic mac Alphurn had finished, Mac Taill applauded vigorously, and he gave vent to other sounds that were clearly those of approval. But Auxilius rose gravely to his feet.

"I cannot," he said, "agree with your interpretation. I desire to do so, but it is impossible. I admit I was impressed when I heard of this Bald Man——"

"I ask you to note," interrupted Padraic, "what I did not perceive till now, that this man was bald. It is true that a bald head is not the same as a shaven head; but a bald head, in the interpretation of dreams and signs, may be certainly accepted as the sign of a shaven head. The sign is even more remarkable than I thought."

"I have noted it," said Auxilius. "I observed it at once. And I say that I was impressed when I figured the Bald Man uplifting the Cup. The picture of this act had a most powerful effect on me. But I saw something else too. I completed the picture, and in my mind I saw the skin of feathers hanging from that part of his body which cannot be mentioned. The symbol was destroyed utterly, for can such a disgraceful thing be imagined, as a sign of salvation to take so obnoxious a form? Therefore, I say that the story must be rejected as an invention, as an indignity, and indeed as a mere temptation of the Evil One to bring our sacred office into ridicule. On these grounds the story only confirms me in my former opinion."

When he had said these words, Auxilius sat down. To have said more would have been to undo their effect visible in Padraic mac Alphurn's countenance. It was clear that the had not thought of the feathers where they were reported to have been placed.

"I am sure," he began earnestly; and then he revised his sentence, strengthening it by self-depreciation: "I am not learned in books, my brethren. I am not, therefore, skilled in criticism, though by the grace of God, to fit me for His Great work, I have been given a natural under-standing without which learning is mere dross. I perceive, therefore, that that part of the story dealing with the skin of feathers is not essential to the tale. It is clearly a later accretion. It is easy to distinguish between the original tale in its purity and the additions of a later scribe moved by the Devil. It is the original tale that has been sent to us for a sign. The skin and feathers are a bawdy addition of the Devil to deceive and mislead us."

"Not so," said Iserninus, rising to his feet. "We must judge the story as a whole. When judged in this way it is seen to be altogether a lewd one. The feathers stuck on this bald man's rump are not the only lewd part of the story. The chaste mind of my brother Seachnall perceived that there had been gross relations between Finn mac Cumhal and the woman Glannluadh. He was checked in a very ill-mannered way by our survival from ancient times, but is it not clear he was right? What brought this woman to accost Finn mac Cumhal on the moun-tain-side?"

"Stay," cried Padraic mac Alphurn; "before we can decide what her part is in the sign we must know what

her name means. Does anyone know what is the meaning of Glannluadh?"

None of them knew, for they were all Galls. The only Gael among them, who should therefore know, was Mac Taill, and he was sunk deep in either prayer or slumber. So they roused him, and put their difficulty to him.

"Glannluadh?" said Mac Taill. "Glannluadh? Glannluadh means Pure Conversation, of course. What else could it mean?"

"I knew it," exclaimed Padraic in triumph. "Glannluadh means Pure Conversation. That must acquit her from your charge, O Iserninus."

"I do not agree," said Iserninus. "The foulest sins mask in the fairest disguises. By deeds, not by professions, must we judge—by deeds and by the purity of doctrine. How immodest it was of her to accost Finn on the mountain-side. And he was led into the bondage of evil by her. Did one ever hear of pure conversation leading men into the bondage of evil?"

"It is by pure conversation that men are brought into the bondage of evil," said Mac Taill, determined now, since he had been aroused, to have a part in the discussion. "Those who know their way about are not so easily caught." But as none knew what he meant, none gave any attention to him.

"The Devil cheats best," said Iserninus, "when he is attired as an angel of light. He may then deceive the very elect——"

"Even so," said Padraic, "if she deceived Finn mac Cumhal, would it not prove him to be elect?"

"Not so," said Iserninus, "for it is the credit of the tale as a sign we must now judge, and we must decide concerning Finn mac Cumhal on other grounds. And so I judge this woman to be lewd. The feathers also are lewd——"

"Why should feathers be lewd?" Mac Taill asked in a pugnacious manner.

"In themselves," said Iserninus, "feathers are not lewd, but in the position described they cannot but be lewd. Therefore I conclude that this story is a lewd story, and for these reasons it only confirms me in my former opinion. For the purity of doctrine cannot be decorated to its destruction by a story that is lewd."

"That," said Seachnall, "could not have been better said. There is no help to be got from this story. Consider only the description of Conan the Bald. Of what is he a type or a sign? If it once got abroad that our holy office had been typified by a figure so gross and unspiritual, there would be an end of all respect. I move the rejection of this story as a sign——"

"Notwithstanding the clear and beautiful symbol of the chalice?" asked Padraic mac Alphurn earnestly.

"It could not have been a chalice or a cup," said Seachnall. "It must have been a mere pagan goblet or bowl. To my mind, the other parts of the story indicate that very clearly. I therefore move the rejection of the story."

"I second the rejection of the story," said Auxilius.

"And I support the rejection of the story," said Iserninus.

Padraic mac Alphurn bowed his head sadly.

VII
THE END OF DEBATE

THEN IT WAS MAC TAILL rose and made the little speech for which he has been so roughly criticised in the margins of all the texts. In the body of the texts it is recorded that he spoke with the air of a man moved to his depths.

"A good story," he said, "is like a good dream. It is pleasant to be remembered, and whether it is a sign of anything or not is of no consequence. And a bad story is like a bad dream, for it is better to forget it quickly and to omit its meaning from mention, if it has any. There are many parts of this story that are memorable. The figure of Conan Maol uplifting this cup with the skin of feathers hanging from his back parts is especially memorable. But the story is also memorable as a whole; and therefore, as a story, it is a good story, and I like it. But in so far as it may be a sign, I am not concerned with it. Directly I suspect a story to have a secret meaning, I desert the teller of that story at once. It is the only thing to do. The other things one could do, all leave a bitter reflection.

"Since you have disturbed me from my meditation, let me say, then, that I like this story well, but not because it may save Finn mac Cumhal's soul. I think Finn mac Cumhal's soul should be saved on quite other grounds. In the first place, I think it should be saved because it was the soul of a human being. Angels may be created as fast as shelling peas, and as like one another, but a soul that has endured the adventure of this life cannot be replaced by all the hierarchies of heaven for interest and companionship. In the second place, I think Finn mac Cumhal's soul should be saved because it is a soul of high quality. All souls are alike worth saving, but all souls are not alike interesting. We must admit this solemn fact. There are good souls that are, all the same, commonplace. We must be careful lest we make too large a collection of this sort. Heaven would be intolerable if it were inhabited wholly by commonplace souls and spirits without experience and with no memories to speak of. Interesting conversation would be impossible, and that comfortable silence, which is the happy overflow of kindred minds, would be forever banished. We must therefore be careful. For there are also souls of high quality. There are rare and well-assorted and richly-refined souls, adventurous and unexpected souls, tragic souls and humorous souls and delicate souls and steadfast souls and souls of simple distinction. Each is good according to its quality, and must therefore be preserved. I see Finn mac Cumhal's soul as a clear and commanding flame, not swayed by the winds of adversity, and causing many other flames, themselves of distinguished quality and colour, to incline towards it. And I say that we cannot afford to lose one soul of that virtue, for such souls are rare.

"Let us, therefore, my dear brethren, distinguish between good stories and good souls. I like the story, but I do not press my liking on anybody. I like it because it is memorable and without meaning. But it has nothing to do with Finn mac Cumhal's soul. That is an entirely separate matter.

"You have said that it is we who must decide as to the end of this soul. I had not thought of that. I had thought this had to do with God. But perhaps you are right. For after all it is we who have the best experience of this earth, and know what is worth preserving in it. It seems to me, then, that Finn mac Cumhal's soul is unlike any other soul, that it is, therefore, irreplacable, and that it must, therefore, be preserved. I move that its proper place is in heaven. I move this on the ground that such a decision is deserving to the quality of the soul and also deserving to the quality of heaven."

During the strange silence that fell on the assembly after these remarkable words, Iserninus rose to his feet. He said:

"I do not agree with anything my brother Mac Taill has said. His words do not savour to me of pure doctrine, and it is by pure doctrine these questions must be decided.

I have already spoken my mind on this matter, and it is unnecessary for me to repeat myself. On the ground of purity of doctrine, which cannot include pagan elements, I decide that Finn mac Cumhal's soul is not in heaven, but that it is already in hell, where it is enduring, and will continue to endure, the torments of the deservedly damned."

Iserninus spoke crisply and sharply, like a man who saw no room for indecision; and when he sat down, Padraic mac Alphurn surprised the assembly by rising to give his voice out of order. He spoke with his glance fixed commandingly on Seachnall.

"With much that my brother Mac Taill has said," he said, "I am in entire agreement. He spoke with Celtic fire and enthusiasm, but the substance of what he said was sound. My voice is that Finn mac Cumhal's soul is in heaven. My voice is given on the ground that we are all sinners, not one worthier than another, and that it is presumptuous to think that God, Who created all alike, should wish so rare a work of His to perish."

"If it were possible," said Auxilius, rising quickly, "for men to get into heaven without entering through the portals of the Church, not one would enter through those portals at all. On the ground of purity of discipline, therefore, my voice is that Finn did not get into heaven because he could not, but that he was, is, and for ever will be, in hell. And lest there be others pressed to that necessity, I urge that this man Oisin, a wanderer in centuries not his own, be instantly informed of this fact, and be requested to give his decision without delay, that he may not share the same fate, and that we may at once continue our itinerary and pursue the quest of souls. We have wasted enough time. There is no time for delay."

Auxilius spoke impetuously, like a man to whom life is too short to accomplish the many tasks entrusted to his care. But Padraic mac Alphurn raised his hand and spoke severely.

"Our brother Seachnall," he said, "has yet to give his voice. If he desires not to, then I will give a casting voice, for the voices are now equal."

So addressed, Seachnall was overcome with earnest thought, to such an extent indeed that he did not notice the intense glances that were directed at him from every side—as was apparent from the circumstance that he did not return any of them. The fate of a soul was being weighed in that thoughtful silence. The excitement was intense, unbearable. Even Iserninus' pale brow was cast with colour, and Padraic's dignity disturbed with anger.

Then Seachnall at last thoughtfully raised himself to his feet, still neglectful of the presence of the others, and delivered himself in these words:

"It is a grave matter, and there is much to say on each side. One never saw this man Finn mac Cumhal, and never had an opportunity of questioning him. In his absence, one can only judge of him by the gross behaviour of his son. Nor does it appear that, lying down or rising up, he repeated for its efficacy a well-composed hymn, or did any charitable work, or that he flayed himself in acts of penitence, or that he esteemed the world as chaff, or that he heard voices and saw visions, or that he bore himself apart from the world in God's righteous election. It is, therefore, difficult to consider him chanting a sweet hymn at all, or otherwise conducting himself as the blessed in heaven do, constantly prostrating themselves before the Eternal Throne, or striking a melodious harp of praise. On the ground, therefore, that the heaven we adore would not be an appropriate place for Finn mac Cumhal, my voice is that he is not there. He cannot be there. I would say he is in hell."

VIII

THE TEMPTATION OF THE DEVIL

THAT NIGHT, PADRAIC MAC ALPHURN lay on the single plank that was his bed. It was so narrow that the least move would have left him on the floor. Sleep would not visit his eyes, for he was sorely tempted of the devil.

From where he lay he could see out into the night. He could see the dome of heaven like a deep-blue robe strewn with wonderful jewels. There was no other light in an infinity of depth but the casual radiance of the stars. Orion rose into the zenith hunting his prey. His bright dog Sirius followed after him over the tops of the trees, his white light dipping in their billowy sea.

From the empty distance the south-west wind halloed through the night in mighty gusts, in bursts of deep-baying music. Padraic mac Alphurn could see the darker darkness of the trees rocking their heads in a mad, wild dance as they stepped to the music of the wind. He heard that music played in a thousand notes as the mad harper stooped from the stars to sweep the long reaches of the woods with his airy fingers. The night was filled with the music. The night was wild with tumult. But the stars were clear and proud and still.

And Padraic saw a man like Finn mac Cumhal walking the hills of Ireland like a giant through the night. He saw him exulting in the wild and proud music, he saw him one with the wild and proud dance. And Padraic saw his brother Seachnall rising to pick his words carefully, and to throw his measured judgment into the swaying balance that was to decide the fate of Finn mac Cumhal's soul. And the devil tempted Padraic mac Alphurn with doubt.

Then Padraic mac Alphurn lifted his knees, and rose carefully from the narrow plank that was his bed. He put the music of the storm out of his ears. He put the sight of the stars out of his eyes. He knelt beside his bed and prayed long and resolutely that he might overcome the devil.

Then Padraic went again into his bed, and slept peacefully and well. And he doubted no more.

THE SIXTH BOOK

I

OISIN AWAKES

As the wind roared through the trees, the leaves laughed and lifted their toes, and danced in companies down secret paths to the nearest open glade. There they circled round each other, swept up and down, parted and joined, hither and thither, in a reel of many parts, but of movements as punctual and faithful as the traditions of leaves are old and the heart of the western harper is young. The full measure always finished with a surge towards the centre, and a spiral movement upwards, high as the tops of the trees, when the oldest in the dance would fly away down the wind, and other companies would come rushing down the secret paths, and the reel would begin again with the first fluttering figure around the edge of the glade.

The most difficult and baffling set swung around Luachra mac Lonan's house, and this was the set that Oisin heard when he woke to meet his faithful comrade the dawn. Yet, no patient observer could have failed to notice how each movement completed itself before another began, whether in eddies over the grassy clearing, or around the corners of the house, or up the walls and beneath the eaves. And all the while they danced they sang a song in thin, shrill, elfin voices, crisp and clear above the noise of the wind.

Oisin heard that song. He also heard the mighty roar of the wind in the woods. The music of each was disentangled in his ears from the music of the other, and the music of each opened his heart so wide with joy that a flood of memories poured into it.

In that grey dawn, the old wonder of the world thrilled his mind. He did not think it a special world made for him; but as it was the only world he knew, he thought it a very good world. He had always accepted it as he saw it, without any previous delusions as to what was right or wrong in it, or what might be better or what might have been worse. It and he, from the first of his days, had been quite virginal in their experience of one another. Neither had tart criticisms ready to make, for neither had set up cantankerous standards for the other, with the result that their hearts had been genial and their minds full of wonder. The geniality had never abated; the wonder had never diminished. At least, thought Oisin, as he listened to the booming chords of the wind and the sharp, shrill voice of the leaves, he could say this for himself, and he hoped, without unduly disturbing himself about it, earth could say it too.

Two hundred years before—it was a long time to look

back over—he had first been brought into the presence of earth by his famous and heroic father. His father! Ah, that father! Such a father! Childlike and wise, happy and grave, simple and fearless in his welcome of all simple and fearless things, proud and wild and unashamed, he had, unlike these bishops, never expected earth to put itself out of the way to suit his preconceptions, or to his son called the ancient attributes of earth by queer and ungainly names. The result was that the thin, slender, metallic song of the leaves still touched him to happiness, and the voice of the western harper thrilled him with pleasure.

And now he was about to leave this world. This very day, as Brogan had explained to him, water would be thrown over him—water specially and mystically prepared, and druidic words spoken—and then no doubt an angel would come on a white horse, singing many Hosannas (which, he understood, was the note of joy for the occasion), and bear him to Finn mac Cumhal and the Fianna of Ireland. Time would accustom him to the Great Whore of Babylon, and he would not mind her at all. So also it would be, no doubt, with the unicorns and the many-headed beasts and birds. The crowds marching one way singing Woe, Woe, Woe, and the crowds marching the other way singing Holy, Holy, Holy, still troubled him a little. Brogan had said the Fianna would not be permitted to hew them in pieces (he had even said the Fianna would not wish to do so, but this was incredible), so that there seemed no remedy. What made Finn mac Cumhal choose such a country at all, he could not think. Yet it would have been gross not to believe Padraic mac Alphurn, who spoke with the dignity and authority that the Fianna had known how to return. And wherever Finn was, there he must also be. Nothing else was to be thought of. For a cloth is only as it is woven, and his weaving had been on the warp of proud tradition and of the woof of sweeter memory.

So this very day he would leave earth of the pleasant winds and woods. He would, it appeared, salute for the last time Ireland of hill and glen, rock and flood, wild and tender and proud. He repeated the music of her place-names with a clean, pure pang of emotion, but without regret; for, the choice having been made, he thought of it no more. Not his to insult a parting with weakness, or to mar a decision with tears.

Indeed, it was timely to leave. Strange things were coming to pass, strange aspects of life being born, which he did not understand, and from which it was his wish to turn his eyes. Even if men had shrunk to being mannikins that was no reason for them to be cowardly and avaricious and ugly. Courage and generosity and beauty were regarded with suspicion, with shame, even with contrition.

Already he heard the morning hymn from beyond the hall—a dismal, mournful note of men determined to be gloomy. The world was certainly changing. Perhaps the berries of the rowan would turn black, and roses change to grey, and colour and beauty fade out of earth herself. That would not be stranger than what he had seen since his return.

It was time to go. He thought with impatience of the wonderful thing that was to happen this day of days. He began desperately to repeat, from end to end, the lesson Brogan had taught him, questions and answers in whole blocks together, without a word misplaced.

II

THE BREAKING OF THE NEWS

IT WAS IN THIS MOOD OISIN came to the assembly that had again been set for his reception. He cleansed his body as he had once done for battle, and he attuned his mind till it was of the temper of his sword— the sword he had left in Tir-na-nOg. And so he stood framed in the doorway a moment, looking on the bishops seated in a circle, before he followed Brogan within the hall.

He noted that none looked at him, and that all their faces were grave. Therefore neither did he look at them, and his face also was grave.

"I am ready," he said, "to proceed to heaven. What is the first thing necessary for me to do to prove myself?"

Padraic mac Alphurn being slow to answer, Iserninus spoke instead.

"The first thing," he said, "is to know the purity of doctrine, which is before all things and above all things. For Finn mac Cumhal is not in heaven. He is in hell. And there also are all the Fianna."

"It is no matter," Oisin answered. "Baptise me, and I will go there. I am impatient to be with them, for there is no goodness apart from them."

This simple and courteous reply had a curious effect on the company, for it seemed to remove from beneath them the order of thought without which speech is not possible. Hence they were not merely silent. They were extremely surprised. It was the practical intelligence of Auxilius that first called order back again, and rallied into impetuous words the dismay that had affected them all.

"Wretched man," he cried. "Do you not understand what it is you are told, that the Fianna are, without exception, in pains and eternal torment?"

It would have been very surprising if Oisin had not heard his cry, but there was no sign to show that he attached unnecessary importance to it. His gravity was not disturbed, or the cool refreshment of his body in any way heated.

"Such a thing is not possible," he said, casually and kindly. "If you but knew them you would say that torment is not for their like. They would not endure it. They would rise up and hew their way out. It would be a very unfortunate thing for any who had a mind to stand in their way." He paused a moment, and then smiled towards the mask of serious intensity behind which Padraic mac Alphurn seemed to have withdrawn. "They would make their way to God," he said, but without letting deference slip into subservience, "and they would all be merry together over their enemies."

Such words as these were more than Iserninus could bear. Their ignorance quickened him more even than their impiety. This must be an excuse for the hasty reproach he had uttered before he knew what he was saying.

"Withered old man, without sense and without reverence," he said, and his voice was unpleasant to hear. "Cease your mad words. It is a marvel to me that God does not wither you where you sit, like a leaf withered in a flame. His forbearance is often unaccountable. Know then that God and the Fianna have nothing to do with one another. For God is in heaven of the highest degree, seated in His majesty, and the Fianna are all in the lowest and most painful circle of fire, being tormented without a moment's ease or respite."

It was then that Oisin lifted himself to an attitude of anger, and rebuked Iserninus in these words:

"If such a thing were possible, then it would be no shame for the Fianna indeed, but great would be the shame for God. For if God himself were in bonds, Finn and the Fianna of Ireland would undertake a war on His behalf, and they would not cease that war until they got the victory for Him. It is not known of Finn mac Cumhal that he ever suffered any man to be in pain or difficulty without delivering him. He would give gold, or he would give silver, or he would give hard battle and lusty blows, but he would not rest until he got the victory for him. For that was the quality that was in Finn mac Cumhal, who was ever generous and gave without asking any return."

The effect of this imperturbable ignorance on Iserninus and Auxilius was both unepiscopal and unfortunate. Iserninus moved his lips, but it was impossible to hear what he said. Auxilius clenched his fists and raised his two arms above his head, so that the wide sleeve of his robe fell to his shoulder and exposed his lean and tireless arms. Iserninus had gone white with surprise, but Auxilius grew red with indignation, and so was the first to speak.

"But," he cried, "do you not understand, O worthless Fian, that it is God Himself who overcame the Fianna and plunged them in the lowest circle of torment? It was with His strength and power He did this, because none can withstand Him, and they were not submissive to His will. Therefore He trod them in the winepress of His wrath."

Now, Oisin was a man who disliked greatly to be addressed in a violent manner, for men conceive such prejudices from the accidents of their training. Therefore his only reply to these words was:

"It was not in the time of the Fianna that that man God lived. Certain it is that whether He were east or west the Fianna would have struck off His head for such intemperateness."

But now Iserninus succeeded in giving sound to the sentence he had already twice framed soundlessly on his lips. It is remarkable to note, as an instance of genuine inspiration, that the thought was the same as his brother had already so capably expressed. For what he now said was:

"God will be avenged on you. He is terrible in His just wrath. All must be submissive to Him."

And Oisin's answer to him came as instant as a sword might have leapt in his hand but a few days before in Tir-na-nOg.

"Finn mac Cumhal," he said, "was not submissive to any man, for he did that which was just, and he was generous of his hand, without favour of him that was next or fear of him that was beyond. Do you not understand what sort of a man Finn mac Cumhal was? Is it possible that you do not know that because he was noble therefore he did right, and not because he was submissive? Finn mac Cumhal could not be overcome, because he had no fear in his heart, and because he gave not for any end but the end that was in the giving. It was the same in all that he did. For no man can be overcome but him that is first in fear, and to be submissive is to propitiate the secret fear in the heart. This shame never darkened Finn mac Cumhal; and if it did, none knew of it, and himself soon forgot it."

And as he spoke these words, Oisin looked at the two bishops in such angered incredulity that, in spite of his monstrous age, they were silenced before the light of his eye—though it is also recorded that their silence was in part due to their total lack of understanding of his strange habit of speech.

"Fear," he repeated, bending down upon them, and driving them further down the steeps of silence, "fear is original darkness; fear is the heart of evil; fear is the dam of monsters; fear is the parent of cruelty; fear is the begetter of lies; fear is many things beside, too numerous to mention, and they are all bad, for fear is the beginning and the end of all crookedness. Do you insult Finn to think he would be fearful and submissive? You will not insult him, then, for it was the training of Finn to forget fear."

Having driven the two bishops to the bottom of the steeps of silence, he turned to Padraic mac Alphurn, who had looked on at this scene behind his mask of serious intensity like a carven image.

"Therefore," he said to Padraic mac Alphurn, in a simple and human appeal, "I wish now to go to Finn mac Cumhal. Baptise me, as you promised, and bring me to him, for I see that the world is not as it was in his time, and wherever he is there would I be also."

III

THE EXPLANATION OF A MYSTERY

APPEALED TO IN THIS WAY, PADRAIC MAC AL-
PHURN put aside his mask of serious intensity, and a soft,
sad smile passed over his face like the shadow of a cloud.
He lifted his hand to touch a tear that stood on his cheek,
and he looked at the wet pad of his finger with great wonder. When at length he spoke, his voice was low in melancholy, and the tender regret of his words made it impossible for one to be angry with him.

"It is doubtless true, O hero," he said, "that the Fianna
were once fearless and mighty enough. But it is no use
arguing, for they are now weak and feeble, and the God
of grace has got the mastery over them."

To him Oisin spoke kindly and friendly, and he said:

"O Phadraic mac Alphurn, if it be the God of grace
spread that report concerning the Fianna, then from this
time out, during all your days, never believe a word He
tells you."

"But it is He," Padraic mac Alphurn said, "that is the
beginning and the end of truth, and without Him there
would not be such a thing as truth at all."

"Then," said Oisin, "someone has borne a sorry tale
of Him. It is not a wise man believes every tale-bearer.
We, the Fianna, never used to tell untruth, and falsehood

was never imputed to us; and as for the bearer of tales, it was his profession, and we were merry over him. Baptise me, and I will go to God and to Finn mac Cumhal, and we will be merry too."

Padraic mac Alphurn looked sadly on Oisin, for it grieved him to think that two centuries of misunderstanding separated him from his pleasant companion. Had himself lived over two hundred years before, he would have wished nothing better than to have been a Fian, to judge by this heroic example; for the heroic conception of life had always stirred his endeavour, and had indeed brought him to Ireland in the beginning. On the other hand, had Oisin been born two hundred years later, what a daring, dauntless companion he would have made for hard days and difficult enterprises. Alas, for the two hundred years between. It was they that made his task now so ungainly and ungracious. His heart was grieved because of those two hundred years. Two hundred years! But no matter.

"O Oisin," he said firmly, "alas, what I tell you now is no falsehood, for it is declared to us in God's own word that those who have not followed His counsel will find a hell of pains their dungeon for evermore."

"Why should they follow His counsel?" Oisin asked him. "Who ever heard tell of Him till now? I never heard of any great feat being done by Him but what you and your clerics spread of His fame. Whereas, Finn mac Cumhal and his proud, illustrious hosts were famous in every land. Is it they who should go into unlikely places seeking for one who was afterwards to be famous for the humming of psalms and the ringing of bells? Indeed, but had you seen them mustered for war, you would not think it of them. Enough for them that their captain was a generous man without blemish, and that they were as like him as it was their luck to be. That was counsel enough for them—that, and to be worthy of themselves."

Padraic mac Alphurn was in desperation. Oisin was not angry, nor was he discourteous; he was merely infinitely removed. Not infinitely removed, perhaps; but this particular and critical two centuries of history was as good as infinity. His wit could not span the infinity of time that lay coiled in the little space that separated their bodies. Their words were the same; but the meanings in them, how different! He tried again.

"O Oisin," he said, and his tone revealed his desperation, "will you never understand? The Fianna were doubtless all that you say. Had I lived in their time I would wish to have been of their company. But they were like the smoke of a wisp, like a little stream in a glen, like a quiet wind on a hilltop, every band of them that were ever in it, beside the august majesty of God, who was from before all time and will be for evermore. There was that amount of difference between them."

Oisin stared at him incredulously, and then quickly controlled himself, for it was part of the tradition of the Fianna, as truthful men themselves, never to look incredulous, whatever their thoughts might be.

"It is doubtless so," he said, "since you say it. In that case, if His degree is higher than theirs, He is now entertaining them, and feasting with them, and they are all merry together. What is the delay that I should join them? I am impatient to go."

Had Padraic mac Alphurn been any other than the man he was, he would have departed from Oisin finally and for ever. He would have left him alone in the house. This temptation, indeed, was present in him; but he quenched it resolutely. His mind said to itself that he would not leave Oisin the only hero in the house.

"Let you not be deceived, O Oisin," he said. "It was I myself told you Finn was being entertained by God. I was wrong. It has been resolved by open voices in a Council that I was wrong, and beyond that it is not possible to go."

"Where is he then?" Oisin asked in sharp anxiety.

"He is sorrowful on a flagstone of pain. He is stretched there with a twist in his head. Scourges are assailing him with poison. And there are no warlike bands coming to his aid."

"And God is no doubt there with him, enduring the same hardship with him," Oisin cried out, leaping to his feet. "Baptise me quickly, and let me come to them that I may rescue them all. Why have you delayed me so long? It was never said of any of the Fianna that they delayed to help a companion."

His excitement was so great that Mac Taill rose to hold him, but he shook him off like a plaything. He stood over Padraic mac Alphurn demanding to be sent on his way, and what with the clamour he made, and the height at which he stood, Padraic found the situation disconcerting and difficult. It was a long time before they managed to get Oisin seated again, so intense was his impatience, but between himself and Mac Taill, with Brogan to help, they succeeded at last.

"Why do you delay me?" Oisin asked in distress. "A moment's grief I would not cause to any man, much less to one so noble as Finn."

"Hear me," Padraic said. "If Finn mac Cumhal is in pains, there is no need why you should be. I desire to save you from the same fate. If you yourself will believe and be baptised, it is undoubted that you may live in heaven in everlasting joy. It is my belief that it is for this you have been kept for these two hundred years in Tir-na-nOg."

"You do not know what you say," and as he spoke, Oisin turned from him. "I would take more delight in the buck of a hound, or in looking at badgers between two glens, than in all the joys of heaven with Finn mac Cumhal in pains. Why does not God, of whom you tell me, rescue him if He is as powerful as you say? Were I by him, and the Fianna, at this moment, I would try to give them speedy help."

Padraic mac Alphurn called upon all his valiance, for

it made him sad-hearted to contend against this ancient pattern of a pagan, with whom he would rather be an ally than struggle against him. The truth had to be told to him. It was the truth he was charged to unbosom. But it was uncommonly stubborn to deliver.

"It is a mystery that is hard to explain," he began; and then he said: "If it were I, I would wish to rescue him. But that is because I am but a man and cannot understand the ways of heaven." He stopped again, while Oisin gazed in bewilderment at him. He looked at Iserninus and at Auxilius, but their faces were stern, and that reminded him that he must not let weakness master him. Humanity was weak. Divinity was strong. He must be strong. He began again.

"It is a mystery. We are not required to understand it, but to receive it. Otherwise it would not be an act of faith, and justification, it is written, is by faith. Faith is the evidence of things not seen, and it is also the belief in things that cannot be proved. Only by prayer and fasting and flagellation can this mystery be known, for it is clearly contrary to all the mind of man has hitherto conceived. That is the proof that it is not of this world, but from heaven. For the wit cannot conceive, nor the mind of man imagine, the things that are from God. They must be internally received."

He glanced at Oisin to see if he were following him, but the blank astonishment visible in that face discouraged him. He felt despair rising like a tide in his heart.

He doubted if even the powerful and subtle intellect of the Blessed Apostle Paul itself would be able to deal with a situation like this, without the support of a prepared epoch in time. He thought vengefully of these two centuries that could remain so impenetrable.

"I do not very well understand you," Oisin said, heroically patient. "Why does not God rescue Finn mac Cumhal? That is what I wish to know."

"Because," said Padraic mac Alphurn, bravely at last, "it is He who has placed him where he is. I will not attempt to explain this to you, because it is inexplicable. God is righteous, and He has placed Finn mac Cumhal on the burning flagstones of hell, and therefore it is an act of righteousness to do this. There is no more to be said. We must only receive it, and for ourselves flee from the wrath to come."

"But Finn would rescue Him if He was in the same condition. Even Goll mac Morna, who was his rival, loved Finn. What should cause God to do such a thing to him as to torture him?"

I V

...AND ITS REMARKABLE EFFECT

FOR A MOMENT, PADRAIC MAC ALPHURN was very bitter against his brethren. If they had only left him alone, instead of insisting on formal councils and purities of doctrine, all might have been well. Oisin would have

been baptised, and these unpleasant explanations avoided.
It was his business to save souls, not to harrow a good
hero's emotions. If he could have once got Oisin to
heaven, who knows what he might have discovered there?
It was much better to leave these things to God, he
thought, as he glanced angrily at Iserninus, instead of
troubling the brain with learned matters of theology. Particularly the brain of an honest pagan like Oisin. As he
had successfully arranged the matter, all had been well;
but there were restless intellects that would make a pattern of the simplest issue. Again he glanced angrily at
Iserninus; and this time he included Auxilius in his
anger. The zeal for organisation could be carried too far
when it included the dead of two hundred years before.
Now, if he were not careful he would lose Oisin. He had
much sympathy with him. He desired to gain him.

"It is a mystery," he said, "and therefore—" He
stopped. He had said that before. He was simply walking
in a circle. Behold the difficulties into which he had been
landed by learned antics. Had not his own natural sa-
gacity, his simple humanity, avoided them rarely? He
tried again.

"You see," he said, "it is in the nature of mysteries
that they should appear unintelligible, but they are not
therefore unintelligent. Let us avoid them, O hero. They
merely becloud the mind. The plain truth of the matter
is that all men are afflicted with original sin, and therefore
are destined to eternal torture."

He looked to see if Oisin had followed him thus far. He saw Oisin staring at him in utmost astonishment. And he heard Oisin say:

"I had not observed this affliction in two hundred years. Am I now to learn of it? And if it is so, then it cannot be helped, and why are the Fianna to be tortured for what they could not help?"

"That," said Padraic firmly, "is part of the mystery, and we must now avoid it. That it is so, is beyond question. Yet in His infinite loving kindness, God did not desire all men to be tortured eternally."

"Only some of them," said Seachnall, and looked for approval towards Iserninus, but Padraic gave no heed to him.

"He therefore devised a plan for saving them. But the virtue of that plan could not be received but by faith——"

"And by purity of teaching," Iserninus said quietly.

"And by joining the Church," said Auxilius emphatically.

"By all these things, at once and together," said Padraic, continuing fearlessly on his way in spite of the clouds he saw gathering on Oisin's face. "You may receive this plan; but as for Finn——"

He did not finish. At this critical point, Oisin, baffled and vexed, cried out in a loud voice:

"But how can He that is less be able to do this to Finn that is immeasurably greater?"

"O Oisin," protested Padraic, with incredible patience,

"have I not told you God is infinitely greater than Finn mac Cumhal?"

"You have said this," cried Oisin in a rage; "but now you say He is less generous, and that His hospitality is less."

"His righteousness is more," Padraic mac Alphurn answered.

"It is not costly and difficult to be righteous," Oisin said. "One need not to be of noble blood to be righteous. Anyone may be righteous by observing the rules. But it is costly and difficult, it is hard of attainment, it is an endowment among few, to be——"

"O Oisin," interrupted Padraic hastily, "it would be unseemly for me to toss comparisons with you. It were blasphemy to do the like, for God is almighty and can be terribly avenged on those who compare Him with others to His disadvantage. We must only compare Him when He comes well out of it. Then comparisons are not blasphemous. Let us therefore avert His anger and speak of His kindness. That, O hero, is assured. He does not desire your destruction but your eternal gladness, and this can only be won by serving His will in everything, as Finn mac Cumhal did not. Be warned by the fate of Finn. Forsake the Fianna, and you will walk with the God of heaven."

Whether it was the intention of Padraic to continue his exhortation is not known. For he stopped. To stop is to do something that cannot be recalled; yet he could not help it. The sight of Oisin swept all speech from his lips and all thinking from his mind. He was horribly aware that the others, though he could not turn to them, had as little control as he over the alarm that crept with slow, white tread over their faces. He would have wished to put his hand over his face to hide that stealthy, steadfast progress, but his hand lay oddly powerless on his knee, where he had last laid it. At the time when he most wanted it for his protection, and to clothe the astonishment that he knew was standing naked in his face, the use of it was denied him, and he could only stare helplessly at the grey eyes of Oisin that brightened before him.

For Oisin was changing. He was changing, yet without a change. He was changing internally, though the external likeness remained the same. There were still a thousand wrinkles about his eyes, but the eyes became the eyes of a beautiful young man. The skin of his face was still tough and yellow like old ivory, but behind that skin a new skin glowed of the fairest complexion. His beard still flowed like a snowy stream, white at the source and yellow at the ends, from his cheeks and chin down over his breast, but it was the oddest, quaintest beard that ever sprouted on a human face. It was the beard of a masquerade. The unseen, yet distantly visible, beauty and youth and vigour glowing behind that face made it seem as if it would any moment drop off in very shame to be there. The skin looked as if it would—indeed, as if it were about to—slough off like a serpent's moult, and reveal the transfiguring beauty being formed (or perhaps reformed) behind it. The thin, long, white hair that fell on the shoulders, growing plump and round, looked like the stupidest wig that ever misfitted its wearer. The very hands, he noticed, grew strong and shapely. There was a hint of unspeakable nobility about the brow, though it was still scored with lengthwise furrows and little delicate crossing wrinkles like the wavering lines of a spider's web. There were hints everywhere. In fact, there were nothing but hints, though hints more persuasive than the resemblance of open day. These were the hints of surpassing beauty, surpassing strength, surpassing grace, courage and dignity.

Padraic mac Alphurn felt dizzy, as if he were falling out of sight. To the end of his days he carried the memory of having seen in a dream a land he knew to be Tir-na-nOg, and that on the shore of that land, beside the margin of the sea, stood a splendid and triumphant Oisin, assured and uncritical and indulgent.

This was his after-memory. Perhaps it was only a delusion. At the moment he could do nothing but gaze in astonishment at the uncanny thing that was happening before his startled eyes. For as the seeming change grew strong in him, Oisin rose to a vast height and began to speak.

V

A MATTER OF TEXTS

IT IS MOST UNFORTUNATE THAT AT THIS POINT the texts vary considerably. They lose the conformity preserved consistently to this moment in an account of important happenings so long ago. The variance is so curious, in fact, that one can only imagine that the faithful Brogan, only source for all the script deckt so bravely on vellum, had been caught in the same net of astonishment as the rest of the company, and wrote afterwards from memory. Even so, the matter remains curious. For the texts, that remain in record, divide in two. One records words that appear to have been spoken by a young man, and the other the words of an old man. They attest the unity of their origin in that they begin the same, are much the same in burthen, and end the same. Their source must have been the same. Their differences, therefore, are alike interesting to the student of the origins of action and to the student of the origins of texts.

It is moreover curious that the value of the texts at this critical moment seem to increase with the degree of their inaccessibility. The great text in the Library at Leipsic, for example, may be examined by all without restriction. Bibliophiles may cluster round it with avid interest beneath the beaming kindness of its custodian. To love books

is the passport to all his treasures and to this the pride of
his collection. But it closes at this point, and gives no
more. Possibly the scribe, who wrote in a beautiful clerkly
hand with few abbreviations, refused to believe the story
any further, and would write no more of it. Who can say?
To this point it is the best of all the texts, the best preserved, the most clearly transcribed, the fullest and most
authentic. Its Gaelic composition, of the oldest form and
with no loan words, is a pleasure to read. It is bound in the
tooled hide of a roan cow. It is a pleasure for an elderly
bibliophile to handle. But alas, it finishes at a loose end.

The text in the British Museum at London is fuller, but
is harder to get at. It is kept in a strong box, and only
shewn to a few, and then only if they can prove, by good
references, that their faith is unimpeachable. Fortunately,
the nature of the faith is not asked, since faith, mere
faith, the vaguer the better, is all that is required in a land
so free. Owing to this it has proved possible to find the
references, and to examine the text watched by the yellow
eye of a hovering attendant—for all ancient Irish texts are
expected to explode into spiritual essences when caressed
with too loving a care. Its binding has been wretchedly
neglected. The pages are better preserved, but they are
written in a crabbed hand, with many abbreviations, and
are difficult to read. Yet it is priceless, for it continues
from this vital moment. It gives the speech of an old man.

The text at Trinity College, Dublin, is hardest of all to
see—even to see, much less to examine. It is kept in a

strong room, underground, at the end of a long, damp, dark passage. A posse of ripe and spruce Fellows, attended by suitable Proctors, mounts guard over it, night and day. It might seem that this care was the fruit of love, but it is believed that this is not the case. One of the Provosts was once known to offer an examination of this precious text to a learned student on the stipulation that he would accord him "first go at all the titbits"; but as this student thought the phrase obscure, the offer was not accepted. Besides which, he was required to take an oath of loyalty and allegiance, and this he was reluctant to do, not knowing to what international complications it might not commit him.

It was only by bribing the most indulgent of the Fellows, and drugging the rest of the posse, that access was got to this precious text. Its binding is damp, and has nearly parted from its pages. It is written in a still crabbeder hand, unbeautiful to see, and is studded with abbreviations. It is, in fact, a hive where the abbreviations of antiquity have swarmed. There is hardly a word in it that is not abbreviated. It is, therefore, difficult to make out, and a joy to the modern bibliophile. But the text is most valuable, and is now used for the first time. It is an accomplishment to have been able to examine it at all. It gives what appears to be the speech of a young man.

These two latter texts, then, are all that help. The speeches of each are given in turn. Students in psychology will mark the curious and subtle differences within a yet

more remarkable framework of identity that attests their
unity of origin.

V I

THE RAGE THAT WAS IN OISIN

IN THE FIRST OF THESE TWO TEXTS, as in the
second, it is recorded that Oisin rose in his standing, vast
and terrific; and that, as he arose, he was transformed internally by the rage that was in him. It is said, too, that he
stood thus for an incredible length of time—a length of
time so incredible that it seemed that time slowed down in
long, heavy throbs and finally at last stood absolutely still,
while the company wondered what was next to happen.
It is said that, as he stood thus, within his grey eyes red
lights shone like camp-fires at a distance within a grey
dusk. And that at last, when to the assembly it seemed
that the roof of day would buckle inward and fall upon
them, these words rushed impetuously towards them from
the hero's lips:

"Is it forsake the Fianna of Ireland, and their mighty
chief, in a time of need? Shame and treachery. It is better
to be faithful, and to be twisted on burning flagstones till
years rot of age, than to drink wine in a cup of dishonour.

"Ochone, O Finn, I will be faithful to you. I will be
faithful to myself. If we cannot resist the fate that is in
store for us, what are we but the memory of a little love, a
little wisdom, a little bravery? And can I go to the end of

time except I carry you with me? I will be faithful to you, O Finn.

"I will be true to our common allegiance. I perceive that victory and defeat are but a chance, and that salvation is a blowing on the scales of truth. Who can avert the future, if omnipotence is perhaps the master? It is better to be true than to be lucky. O Finn, I will be true to our allegiance.

"Be of good heart, O Finn. If you are now in pains, those who knew you loved you. Unjealous you were, generous you were, wise and gentle and as lucky as you could be. To be lucky is not to be worthy, for men are the sport of jealous gods. The high-mettled steed is the pack-horse, and the common jade is stalled. Be of good heart, O Finn.

"O Finn, be of good courage. The fruits of victory are with deceit and bribery. To those who have will be given, and from those who have not will be taken away. Yet victory is not in the fruits, but in the unbreakable will. We can resist yet, O captain. It is better to be tortured than to bend the knee. Be of good courage, O Finn.

"The world is a dream, O Finn. The world is a dream of our hearts. We can make it and mould it, O captain, according to the shape of our will. With truth, with courage and love, hard it would be not to triumph. And if we are broken at last, the world is a dream, O Finn.

"Proud was the strong band of our companions. Pleasant our companionship. What are we but our memory of one another, and the memory of our mighty enterprises? Goll mac Morna the unruly, Caoilte mac Ronan the gentle, Conan the Bald, uncouth and cowardly, Oscar my son, the brave, Daire of the sweet-sounding music, and little Cnu of the slumberous songs. And a thousand others besides. O proud was the strong band of our companions.

"Where we have loved we are one. We are only what we have remembered. The wave of Rughraidhe lashing the shore, the lowing of oxen in Maghmaoin, the seagull's scream in distant Iorrus. The murmur of the streams in Sliabh Mis, the yell of the hounds at Drumlis, the noise of the fawns round Sliabh gCua. The hound's deep bay at twilight's fall and the barque's sharp grating on the shore. For where we have loved we are one.

"What am I here or hereafter but the love I gave you, O Finn, and the love you gave back to me? The silent regard of gentle Caoilte is part of my soul for ever. The rough strength of Goll mac Morna, who can take it away from my own? What we have taken and what we have given is woven secretly together. Who will part them? Who will disjoint them? And what am I here or hereafter, but the love I gave you, O Finn, and the love you gave back to me?

"The world is changed, O Finn. Generosity is now a weakness where we were generous and strong. It is wise now to run and be saved when we were wise and prepared for disaster, calm and with courage unbroken. Honour is now of dishonour. Shame is the rule of life, for men are ashamed of themselves. The world is changed, O Finn.

"Yet I will be faithful to you. I will be faithful to myself. To desert you I would be ashamed, and would immediately fall from myself. What is proper for you will be good for me, for what is good for me would be proper for you. If we cannot war with our hands we can war with our wills to the end. I will be faithful, O Finn.

"Ha, are you in pains, O Finn? I will rescue you. I will be strong for you. I will pluck down the banded stars. If it is true that vengeance and wrath are the last will now to be met, then we will open old wars, my captain. I will come to you at once, that we may free captives, and extend hospitality, O mighty one. I will break through the gates of your dungeon. I will tear up the flagstones of hell. I will free you from pains, O Finn.

"Ochone, O Finn, I will be faithful to you."

VII

THE SPLENDOUR OF OISIN'S LOVE

IN THE SECOND OF THESE TEXTS, as in the first, it is recorded that Oisin rose in his standing, shining and wondrous; and that, as he arose, he was inwardly transfigured by the splendour of his love for Finn. It is said, too, that he stood thus for so great a length of time that the company was raised to an incredible excitement—for it seemed that slow time was quickening its flight so swiftly that it became a reeling flutter of hours and years until time had ceased to be, its cycle full completed. It is said that, as he stood thus, within his grey eyes a gathering brightness shone like the rising of the sun beyond the grey dusk of dawn. And that at last, when to the assembly it seemed that, dizzy and fearful, they must fall from the unattainable heights to which they had been carried, these words poured melodiously forth from the transfigured hero's lips:

"Is it forsake the Fianna of Ireland, and their great chief, in time of need? Shame and disgrace. Sweeter to be faithful in torment and torture than to sit at a feast of dishonour.

"Airiu, O Finn, I will be faithful to you. I will be faithful also to myself. We will go forward to the end of time together. Whatever fate may be in store for us it will not part us, but we will carry together the memory of our tender love, our gathered wisdom, our happy bravery. I will be faithful to you, O Finn.

"I will be true to our common allegiance. It is better to be true than to be lucky. For what is victory but a chance, and what is defeat but a chance also? To fall is but a chance, and to survive is but a chance. It is all a chance. But to be ready, unafraid and well-equipped is to be true and also to be lucky. I will be true to our common allegiance, O Finn.

"Be of good heart, O Finn. If you are now in pains, the luck will turn. For you are high in our hearts, O captain. There you are victor still. Jealousy never clouded your heart, and they who came to you empty went full away. Wise, gentle and beauteous you were, and the thought of you is richer than gold. For what is it to be lucky but to be worthy, since the gods are the sport of men? Can the high-mettled steed be the pack-horse or the common jade be stalled? Be of good heart, O Finn.

"Be of good courage, O Finn. The fruits of victory are to the strong, and the ripe fruits to the brave. To those who have will be given, and from those who have not will be taken away. So we will fight on, O captain. It is better to be tortured than to bend the knee. For victory comes at last to the unbreakable will. Be of good courage, O Finn.

"O Finn, the world is a dream. The world is a dream of our hearts. We will make it and mould it, O captain, according to the shape of our will. Truth on the lips, courage in the heart and strength with the right hand, and we will triumph at last. For the world is a dream, O Finn.

"Proud the strong band of our companions. We will renew our pleasant companionship. We will renew our tender memories. We will continue mighty enterprises. I greet my gay companions. Goll mac Morna the boisterous, Caoilte mac Ronan the tender, Conan the Bald, the clumsy, Oscar, my own brave Oscar, Daire of the sad-sounding music, and little Cnu of the sleepy songs. I greet the thousand others. For proud the strong band of our companions.

"We are one where we have loved. We will rove the pleasant places. We will hear the pleasant sounds. The wave of Rughraidhe lashing the shore, the lowing of oxen in Maghmaoin, the seagull's scream in distant Iorrus. The murmur of streams on Sliabh Mis, the yell of the hounds at Drumlis, the noise of the fawns round Sliabh gCua. The hound's deep bay at twilight's fall and the barque's sharp grating on the shore. We are they, they are we, O captain. We are one where we have loved.

"What am I here or hereafter but the love I give you, O Finn, and the love you give back to me? Can I not see Caoilte looking tenderly at me? The bold strength of Goll mac Morna is waiting for me. It is coursing in me expectant. I am coming, my brave companions, too long we have been divided. We give and we take, we take and we give, and we are all woven secretly together and cannot be parted for ever. For what am I here or hereafter but the love I give you, O Finn, and the love you give back to me?

"The world is changed, O Finn, but what is that to us? If generosity is considered a weakness, we will be generous and strong. We will not run to be saved. We will be ready for disaster, calm and with courage unbroken. With us, honour will ever be first, and we will not be ashamed of our deeds, though the world is changed, O Finn.

"I will be faithful to you. I will be faithful also to myself. To desert you is not to be thought of, either for you or for me. We will bear the one load together, we will share the common bed. We cannot choose our fate, but we can choose to be faithful. Yourself that taught us, O captain. And we can choose, and we will, to war with our hands, to

war with our hearts, and to war with our wills to the end.
I will be faithful, O Finn.

"Ha, are you in pains, O Finn? I will rescue you. I am
strong for you. I defy the unlucky stars. We will open new
wars, O captain, on the vengeance and wrath of the gods.
I am coming to you, O mighty one, in order that we may
free captives and extend hospitality. I will break the gates
of your dungeon. I will tear up the flagstones of hell. I
will free you from pains, O Finn.

"Airiu, O Finn, I will be faithful to you."

VIII

THE DISAPPEARANCE OF OISIN

THESE WORDS are remarkable that they appear
in both texts in difficult poetic structure. Even in the
heroic days of the speaker (not to speak of the sub-heroic
days of the hearers) men did not address one another in
poetry in the ordinary, or in the extraordinary, moments
of their lives. They set aside, and gravely or wildly honoured, special people to indite poetry for them, and sometimes to them.

It must be, therefore, that this fierce and splendid
moment can only be perceived by us through Brogan's recollection in tranquillity. It cannot be hoped to measure the
effect of this terrific outburst on the assembled company.
All that is known is that they all recovered from their

utter stupefaction to see the decayed Luachra mac Lonan rise in his place and cry in an agonised voice: "My captain, my hero, my warrior," and fall forward in a swoon from which he died the same day.

But when they looked round to find Oisin they could not see him. Where he had gone, how he had gone, none could say. Each man asked his fellow, but his fellow knew no more than he. None had seen him go. It must be that while they sat stupefied he had left them to find Finn mac Cumhal and the Fianna of Ireland.

Had Luachra mac Lonan seen him go? Was this why he had risen and cried out despairingly? Poor decayed warrior, he never recovered to answer these questions.

THE SEVENTH BOOK

I

WINDS OF RUMOUR

What befell Oisin after he left Luachra mac Lonan's house has never been known for certain. It is true, rumour has flown thick with tales; but, as usual, these tales are often preposterous, and where they are not preposterous, they destroy one another. It is impossible, in an episode of such importance in the history of a nation, and the onward carrying of faith, not to be too scrupulous in submitting every source to the most exhaustive examination. Mere rumours are barred at the very frontiers of the enquiry.

It can be seen how important this moment was considered to be by the mere fact that, in addition to the sources that have already been mentioned, four rooms at the Royal Irish Academy are piled thick, from floor to floor, with manuscripts dealing only with this point. What happened to Oisin when he left Padraic mac Alphurn? Did he perchance die in the faith, or did he possibly die out of it? Did he repent, or did he not? Was he saved, or was he not? To what kind of an end came he, and what did he think of all he had heard? These are vital questions. Witness the four roomsful of manuscripts, piled thick from floor to roof, that have been deemed worthy to contain the answers.

All these had to be closely examined. It is true that many of them only contain rude remarks that have not much practical bearing on the question. Some of them contain obscene jests, in difficult Irish or still more obscure Latin. Others are filled with drawings that are perplexing to understand. Some of these drawings are of plumed and mysterious presences, but more of no kind of presences at all.

These must be put to one side. They cannot, no matter how carefully they are examined to find an inner meaning, be made to help. There still remain about two roomsful, and from an exhaustive search through this material, and a careful collation of each with each, crossing out all rumours that cancel one another, the following few incidents drop through the finely meshed sieve of criticism, and may therefore with authority be dropped on this page.

It is said of an old man who lived in the clusters of houses at the foot of the hill where now Rathfarnham is, that he came out to see from the sunset what sort the morrow would make. He returned more rapidly than he went, and sat by the side of his log fire with an awed expression on his face. His wife, noticing his strange behaviour, asked him what was amiss. He replied that he had seen coming

down the hill, apparently borne on the effluence of the sunset, a strange and wonderful being, vast of height, with
snowy-golden hair falling on his shoulders, and a brightness flowing from about him that was like the brightness
of fish newly caught from the sea. He had barely reached
the dyke when he saw this being striding beside the margin
of the forest, yet barely touching the earth with his toes;
and he had not waited to see more, but had hastened within
the house, for it was not seemly to be too curious when
the gods were abroad.

She then had agreed with him. They had both agreed
with one another that good times must be coming again
to the country now that the gods were flying on the effluence of the sunset and revealing themselves to men.
And they had spent the rest of that night speaking of the
good old times of which his father had told him.

It is said of a young man who stood that night at the
gable-end of his house interestedly gazing out towards the
forest-clad hills in the dusk by the village at the southern
end of the ford of hurdles that spanned the Liffey, where
it meandered down through the bog on its path to the
sea, that he, too, suddenly entered the house and sat by
the fire of dried turves with a pale and frightened face.
He had never been known to do this before. His interest
in the forest-clad hills, at all hours of light and darkness,
had ever continued unabated till it was time to forget
them in sleep. Therefore his mother had asked him what
was amiss.

With difficulty he told her that he had seen a terrible demon stalking the road towards the ford. Mysterious fires gleamed from his eyes. His hands had been flung over his head in wild gesticulations of triumph over humanity. His breast was open and revealed the unearthly fury that possessed him, while lightnings played about his head. So she had caressed him, and together they had prayed that no ill might befall them, and that they might be shielded from harm, but they had remained awake all night in terror, notwithstanding.

It is said that a mild and mature Dane, of the little Danish establishment where now Cluain Tairbh is, went out at night to make sure that his boats were well beached when he felt the wind shift to the south; but that he had hardly left the house when he returned again, and sat by the dying fire of drift-timber with a thoughtful expression on his face. His wife, who was already in bed, turned to look at him in the dim light of the fire before she asked him what was amiss.

He told her that he had seen a strange being, who was either one of the gods of the land, or one of the old sort of Irishman of whom he had heard; but that it was indifferent to him which it was, for, either of them, it boded no good for Danish establishments by the sea. He accepted it as a bad omen. An ill thing would certainly happen to the Danes at Cluain Tairbh, mark his word.

To this she answered that there was no accounting for the queer ways of men. Being irritable and sleepy, she

asked him were the boats well beached. And he had replied stubbornly that he would go out no more that night,
boats or no boats.

II

THE PASSING OF OISIN

ALL THOSE INCIDENTS are well established, and
they shew the way Oisin went after leaving the assembly.
They indicate his path with beautiful precision, like the
footprints of an otter. But there is one other incident
that closes the series. It was found in an old hagiology,
that had almost been overlooked, for it is the one priceless truth in the century of credulous fables that en-
cumber its pages.

It is said that one morning (by exact synchronism it
proves to be the morning succeeding to the incidents already related) a young and vigorous herd went out with
the break of day to tend his care along the wild bluff of
Benn Edair. He went along the southern side of the bluff,
singing a new hymn he had learnt; but, feeling gay and
happy so early in the morning, he marred his rhythm by
singing it too jauntily.

Suddenly he lifted his head, to see emerging from the
forest that clothed the headland a wonderful being that
strode towards the shore. At first he was uplifted, for he
thought that a vision was being vouchsafed him. For the

being was fairer and more beautiful than anything he had
ever seen. It was tall above the manner of men, and more
supple than their wont. Looking on that being, he was
proud to be young, and glad to be in life. Its clothes were
strange, and strangely frayed and old, but its face was like
the dawn. Striding downward to the sea in those ancient
but richly embroidered garments, this being was like the
sun breaking through the rags of clouds that would obscure its dawn.

So the young herd hid himself in a clump of heather to
see what would happen; and he saw this wonderful being
leap over the beach, where the waves thundered on the
shore, and enter the waters, and battle proudly and, as it
were, lovingly, with the waves. This frightened the young
herd so much that he at once hid his face in the clump of
heather, so that he could not see what happened. But in a
moment he heard these mysterious words ring like beautiful bells across the morning air:

"Mannanán mac Lir!"

When he looked again there was nothing to be seen.

He confessed these things to a saint who lived on roots
nigh handy, and the saint told him he had seen a demon.
He asked if this was an omen that he would die by drowning; and the saint told him that he would not die by
drowning if he never went near water. So that he did
penance and went to live inland, and ever afterwards
avoided water as he was counselled.

III

THE BLOCK OF GRANITE

SOME DAYS after this in Gleann-na-Smol through a path in the woods a slow procession wound its way. It was led by little children in white robes, whose shrill voices sang a solemn tune with a slow and regretful cadence. These children were followed by bearded men, also in white robes, whose deep voices blended and were mingled with the piercing tones that the children sang.

Other men followed, who wore heavily and sumptuously brocaded vestments over their white robes. They walked with slow and deliberative tread, as well they might, for the procession was shaped about them, as a ring is shaped about the jewels to uphold which it was designed.

First of these came Padraic mac Alphurn, Primate of all Ireland. He walked with grave and dignified aspect, his grey eyes shining like a well tempered sword. Behind him walked Bishop Seachnall, otherwise Secundinus, a small, old man, with alert questioning face; Bishop Iserninus, otherwise Fith, a man of thin lips and austere brow; Auxilius, Bishop of Cill Usaile, a man broad in the cheek-bones and likewise broad in the brow; and Mac Taill, Bishop of Cill Culainn, great and powerful of build, and gentle and soft of aspect. Seachnall looked

pensive, Iserninus reflective, Auxilius thoughtful, and
Mac Taill gloomy.

The procession wound on its way, and rested, coiled
around a block of granite that was hewn square and
trimmed craftily and stood exactly in the corner of a
great clearing where the sod had been cut away to its bed
of gravel at the base of the mountain-side. It lay grey and
comely in the soft evening light, shining against the
orange gravel clearing where the pale green verdure had
been cut away. It was the cornerstone of the new church,
and the five bishops gathered thoughtfully about it.

"It is a good position," Padraic mac Alphurn said
at last.

"It is a proper and suitable position," said Mac Taill.
"I like it. And that," he added in a deep and mellow voice,
"is a most excellently shapen piece of stone. I like that,
too." But it was noticed that he was not paying very particular attention either to the clearing that had been cut
or to the granite that had been hewn.

"We cannot continue the church," said Iserninus then
in a clear, relentless voice.

"Why cannot we continue the church?" Padraic mac
Alphurn asked sharply, looking round him in surprise.

"We cannot continue a church the corner-stone of which
was laid by a pagan," Auxilius said from the other side
of him.

When Padraic mac Alphurn turned to the other side of
him, Iserninus added from this side of him:

"And a pagan who rejected the true teaching when he heard it."

And when Padraic mac Alphurn turned back again, Auxilius spoke from the other side once more.

"One who himself refused to enter the church," he said. "We would be held up to laughter for ever if we built a church which he who laid the foundation stone himself refused to enter. It is not to be thought of. The building must be abandoned."

"I entirely agree," Seachnall affirmed. "The place is accurst. It is a most fortunate circumstance that the ground was never consecrated."

A great sadness clouded Padraic mac Alphurn's noble features. He had himself nourished the thought that this cornerstone would remain to him for a memory of a man whom his mind held with an appealing tenderness. But no one could deny the strength of these arguments, especially as they were enforced by a clear majority.

"I had not thought of that," he said coldly. "We will return the way we came." And he waved his hand to the procession.

"It is a pity," said Mac Taill, turning away. "But no matter. The stone will not be easily removed. It will remain for a memory of Oisin for ever."

NI BEAG SAN.